D1738966

1

Recently by Marcus Sanford

THE NERVE
novel and script

Does evil get the last say?

If there is only one kind of miracle, or if there are none at all, then we are all stuck thinking 'if only, if only…' for the rest of our lives. Yet there are those around us with far more wrenching situations than ourselves whose 'miracle' is their strength of character. Follow three people in modern times as they wind their way through a maze of modern pretense—the beliefs that there are no miracles at all, or that only one pre-conceived outcome is miraculous.

At Amazon.com/books

Youtube: The Nerve script demo

"This script is awesome. I've got to do this. I totally enjoyed the changes of direction late in the story…" -- Jeannie Garcia, actress, OPEN MY EYES, 2016

"When I got the book, I noticed several blank pages at the back, and the story had such an impact on me that they are all full of my own journal now. At least, I thought that was what they were for!" --Amanda, vocalist, mother

Novels, scripts by Marcus Sanford

DELUGE OF SUSPICIONS
INTERCEPT (formerly FOOTHOLD)
THE NATION OF SCARFACE
SENSELESS
SILENCE FOR BREGE

At Amazon.com/books

Video demos at Youtube:

THE NERVE (with Hillsong's "What A Beautiful Name")

SENSELESS (with Hillsong's "Rain Down")

'All Lives Matter – Marcus Sanford'

The video of historical background of MORE OF THE SAME is at Marcus Sanford Be Careful What You Wish For documentary

More
Of The Same

a novel
Marcus Sanford

(previously titled DESOLATED)

To Western Cons. Bap. Seminary,
A powerful untold event in
apologetics.

5

— *[signature]*

Jual. 2024

MORE OF THE SAME (previously titled DESOLATED)
Marcus Sanford, October, 2016; May.12.18; all rights reserved
ask@interplans.net, 360-460-9473
PO Box 1074, Sequim, WA 98382

Thanks to the following test-readers!
Jolinda Creary, Rodney Kashmir, Audrey Ellen, Amanda Fiorini,
Kari Christenson

CONTENTS

Foreword

Some of my Master's degree research was on the impact of British evangelicals in the thick of the threat of revolution. For all its coverage of the battle against slavery and against the tightness of capital for improvements for lower classes, my research and guides at that time missed a rather exciting episode.

This episode took place in the early years of the 1800s and through the teaching of a Pastor George Holford. There is very little material available on the person or his family; most of the time, an inquiry will be guided toward a better-known attorney and relative of the time.

However, I was struck to learn that the attorneys who had earlier defended a publisher of Paine, Erskine and Kyd, were later representing the Crown *against* Paine and among the support for their case was the teaching of Holford. By 1805, Holford's treatise was published. It is unfortunately in the complex English of that period that reminds us of The Declaration of Independence or the Constitution.

Even so, Holford's presentations and publication made a significant impact on England: Reform? Yes. Revolution? *No.*

Not only had Holford scored in defense of the reasonable truth of Scripture on the mainstage of history, he had shown what one wild fanatic revolution had become.

This was no small talking point, because Edward Lennox , who was raised in the queen of Ireland's household, more by his household gardener than by his father, was to become a radical trying to help Paine's effort in England. Edward, his mother recalled after he died of a British security force's gunshot wound, was always talking about the garden of Eden. Because revolutionaries want to create *a new Eden*, they yawn at trying to reform a London or Athens in our world where there is the problem of human evil to deal with. The French Revolution, for example, started its world clock at year 0.

Although this story's young radical Fitzwilliam does not refer to Edward, he was modeling him in preparation for Paine's plans for England. Fitzwilliam, Millie, Elnora, Martin and Tilson's Park are fictional, and some events of the time have been adjusted a few years or miles for impact in the story. The location of this Holford family is, as mentioned above, not clear. What is clear is that evangelical Lord Shaftesbury had a huge impact in housing in London and was as clear a voice as Wilberforce was about slavery. One of my master's research papers was based on reading THE TIMES on how the construction developed.

Tellson's was a major bank of the time; *Tilson's* was created here to show how money started to be used for benevolent investing.

In the back of the book, there is a list of Places and People, and descriptions followed by an "H" are actual historic figures.

At certain points, the reader of DESOLATED may think there is some problem with the American Revolution, but actually the problem is the term 'revolution' back in England. There was the backdrop of the horrid illustration of what revolution could mean across the Channel. The Americans wanted and secured *independence.*

There could always have been more effort for independence of lower classes, and sooner, in England, but the point here was to show the Evangelical effort toward it, combined with Holford's stunning presentation to the public about the 'Great Revolt' in Judea and its ruination of that country. Although Paine had initially been inspired by the Galatians 5 sermon he heard in Philadelphia, the British public realized through these efforts that the humorous wit of Paine was not reliable about the truth of the Bible. The lower classes also saw through the inflammatory rhetoric that cited them to invade and seize the properties of those who were landed.

Personally, I was most surprised in this research to find the intention of Paine when pushing 'the vote.' It's good that he was approaching change without violence, but it was *intellectually* violent (in the same sense as the expression 'intellectually dishonest'). He once said that he had the same beliefs as the un-armed Quakers, except that his beliefs *were* 'armed.' And referred to 'platoons' of philosophers ready to go to work on the English public.

All this to say that Paine's model was way too close to the insipid modern Democratic party push to have illegals and minors down to age 16 be given voting powers. To the English public at the time, Paine's proposal that all men vote was intellectually dishonest, and in the Colonies, only self-employed men voted at first.

Marcus Sanford, April 2018

HISTORICAL NAMES AND PLACES

H = historical figure

Beachy Head. Another name for the Ditchling area.

Brighton. A coast city due south of London.

Bourneboro Estate Home for Children in Brighton. A house donated by the Bourneboro family to Holford for children.

Carsten, Benjamin. Lightman mistakenly killed by Summers.

Ditchling. Site of highest light station above Brighton.

Duche. Pastor in Philadelphia who teaches Galatians 5, heard by Paine. H

Erskine, Thomas. Attorney who represents the Crown vs. Thomas Williams who published Paine and is deeply impressed by Holford's teaching. H

Evans, Jane. Novelist with bizarre marital life regretted at the end. H

Everton, Miles. Reading Paine.

Holford. George, father, pastor; Martin, son, in pastoral training. Loves Elnora, governess of Bourneboro Home.

King's Coaches. Pub and transit center.

Lennox, Edward. Son of Duchess of Lominster who fought in America and returned changed, studied under Paine, and assisted Irish and others in revolution against the Crown. H

Merrimount, Kathryn. A woman working at Slickson's who had visited Holford's Brighton church and helps Millie recover from her forced abandonment.

Millie __. Young girlfriend of Summers forced to abandone a newborn by Fitz.

Picking, Elnora. Daughter in Holford's church who supervises the new orphanage.

Pruitt, Abner. Lightman, inconclusively witnessed Millie at the beach.

Paine, Thomas. British-born American and French political mover. H

Slicksons Farm. Initial 'safe' location for Summers and Millie. In Uckfield, NE of Brighton.

Summers, Fitz. Student of Paine, firebrand, penniless, illiterate.

Sussex. South coast region including Eastbourne, Brighton, Hastings.

Tilson Park Estate. A farm property belonging to Lord Tilson, an evangelical who seeks to use it for housing while saving the center of it for farm production.

Uckfield. Remote town in Sussex, south coast.

Williams, Thomas. Publisher of Paine in England, put on trial. H

Woodland, Mathew, Greta, Sharon, etc. Orphans who are sent by mother's dying wish to Brighton to the Holfords.

TIMELINE

DESOLATED is based on the following historical events

1775 Paine hears Galatians 5 preached by Duche

1776 Paine's contempt for OT first expressed, printed

1783 Paine in NYC

1789 Confiscation of church property in France

1792 Paine deported from England under threat of execution

1792 Most vocal French opposition to divine right of kings

1793 Execution of Louis

Rickman convicted for publishing Paine COMMON SENSE and THE RIGHTS OF MAN in England

Paine in hiding in France

French preparation for invading England

Notre Dame renamed Temple of Reason

1794   AGE OF REASON published

Robespierre arrested by the National Assembly

Coup of the Committee for National Safety and disbanding of it

1795   The French Directory, return of many bourgeoise values

1797 Trial of Thomas Williams for publishing AGE OF REASON, England

1804   Bonaparte as Emperor of France

1805   Holford's treatise on the Destruction of Jerusalem

1831 Darwin sails to Galapagos

THE
DESTRUCTION
OF
JERUSALEM.
AN ABSOLUTE AND IRRESISTIBLE
PROOF
OF THE DIVINE ORIGIN OF
CHRISTIANITY:
INCLUDING A NARRATIVE OF
THE CALAMITIES WHICH BEFEL THE JEWS,
So far as they tend to verify
OUR LORD'S PREDICTIONS
RELATIVE TO THAT EVENT.
WITH A BRIEF DESCRIPTION OF THE
CITY AND TEMPLE

"I consider the Prophecy relative to the destruction of the Jewish Nation, if there were nothing else to support Christianity, as absolutely irresistible."
(Mr. Erskine's Speech, at the Trial of Williams, for publishing Paine's Age of Reason.)

Stereotype Edition.

EXETER, N. H.
PUBLISHED BY LEONARD JACKSON.
1830.

The opening page of Pastor Holford's material when published in 1830.

1
Walking to Tilson's

The road from Uckfield, near Brighton, Sussex, England, 1798
Matthew Woodland held the hand of his nextborn sister, Greta, who held the hand of the next, on down to the youngest of the 6 Woodland children. The little orphaned band moved along as slow as the youngest would allow until they took turns picking him up.

"When will we see the Tilson Estate Emparkment?" asked Greta.

"And what does it look like?" answered Matthew. He shrugged, but guided them with his smile. "That's no matter. Our parson said to find the evangelical church as you come into Brighton. That's the place. Ma had written to them about us."

"What is an '*em-park-ment*?" asked Sharon in the middle.

Matthew took a stab at it. "It's nicer than a farm."

"But at least there is food at a farm" answered Greta.

"But there will be fish in Brighton! And chipped potatoes!"

"Ugggh—Fish." moaned Greta. "Chips and cheese for me."

"Hey, Greta, do you know how to eat fish?" teased Matthew.

"No."

He pinched her nose shut and said "Now, chew!" And they all laughed. Except Greta, who slapped him back.

"Yes, but we won't worry, you hear" led Matthew. "We won't. It's not good for the soul. We've been led this far, and we prayed with him when we left. God will guide; he'll provide. And besides, all these people in a city like Brighton, they all have their gardens, sometimes in the country, I've heard. And they will need helpers.

"But there'll be no thieving, do you understand? It's disorderly and means you have no hope. That's no way to live. We'll always offer to work. That's good, wholesome knowledge, and honors our ma and da. And then we'll always know these things ourselves—how to take care of this or that animal or plant. And we'll get paid for that."

For age 16, he had a remarkable way of inspiring the young ones. "Ma always had hope, no matter what the news. Yeah, she had lots of pain, but at the end, she knew God would watch over us, and she had her last smile—" and here Matthew choked back tears recalling that last scene with mother.

Greta gripped him closely and they saw a sign that Brighton was now just 3 miles away.

"Why is it called Brighton?" one of them asked.

"Sunlight" answered Matthew.

Philadelphia, 1775
Pastor Duche was just hitting stride in his presentation.

> What is our experience in this new world? Isn't it quite the same as what the apostles spoke of in the decisive letter to the Galatians, in 5: 'It is for freedom that Christ has set us free.' What could be plainer? And thus here we are in a new world, a free people, being asked by powers and authorities with whom a conversation takes months to go even one round, to pursue some other course.
>
> And now we hear of the threat of military force coming to our shores, the shores of a free people, to impose what those authorities said should be—or said should be 4 months ago!
>
> But freedom is in Christ for the Christian, and in civic things, it is in God, not a state. It is not the state that supplies it, but God the Creator, even if a person is not a Christian. And what the state does not supply, it cannot retract!

The audience was stirred and concerned. How close could he come to a call to arms—*without* a call to arms?

Thomas Paine listened to Duche and sat rather struck as he concluded. He had often considered sermons to be the most stimulating time of the week—but not necessarily because of the preacher's topic! Sometimes it was some other nagging issue. Or it might be an angelic face off to the far left from where he was sitting, who always seemed to look away just as he checked. Especially in these months after his wife had died in childbirth.

Nagging issues. Even more so since coming to the new world. He had his problems with the Bible, but not with this message today. This was the pure stream of water from which every civilized person should drink.

Thomas Paine needed to be absorbed in that new world—in its *birth,* because of the way his poor wife had died. He needed a new beginning. He did not need the image of his trouble back in England. He needed to move on.

After a good lunch with Caleb Hinckley, the fellow renting one of his rooms, he fell asleep. That afternoon, he meditated his way through that passage of Galatians. He noticed the 'return to slavery'. How Paul's opposition was going to make those free people slaves *again.* Where was that from? And today, why was England the 'plague of the world'? Why were monarchs and prelates of churches 'enslaving again'?

But it was a gift from God that he slept only for a moment. It was a deep recharging sleep and then he found himself waking to new, wonderful phrases about a government structure that could preserve liberty for good. A set of three 'powers'. One for writing what few laws would be needed, one for policing those, and a third that was a person or maybe three who would take a turn at presiding over any conflicts that came up; yes, a *president* or a presidium. To give government a truly personal face, but not an individual "god." Not that pompous '*Mad*-jesty' that inherited his position for life, they said, direct from God. A bit too direct, he thought, as did his fellow-dissenters. Not the circus act Paine had portrayed in his writings, at which most people would burst in cynical laughter as he pulled the curtains back to show how the 'puppet' was operated.

He found Caleb off in some other pursuit as he read by his fire. "Listen to this:

Resolve that there be three branches of power in our government, and one of those be three parts.

A house approving laws for the populace, a house enforcing those laws and bills, and a presidium of three of the wisest of those houses to resolve conflicts and act executively in cases calling for quick response to the affairs of the country.

Caleb summarized what he heard: "Legislative... judicial... executive... I notice you started at the populace's end of things, and you have no individual in power—if you can help it."

"Exactly. And even they take turns."

It was only a paragraph, but it was *revolutionary.* It was worth fighting for.

'*Taking turns.*' He chuckled in delight. It reminded him of a dance at a ball, not only that the job description of this person was in place, but also their length of service to the people. A few years at most; one dance at a time. Not the same girl all evening. It was about taking turns, because there is evil all around, and there are no 'divine' monarchs.

"But if there is evil all around, how large will your 'legislative' house be? Do you really want 100 of them to gather?"

"I want a proposal to survive all three branches. That is what checks evil *within.* But I also want a 'presidium' to check evil *from outside.* And act as one."

"You could save money."

"Money? I'm not sure there will be any money. But there must be money for an army."

Caleb concluded: "I would not make it any larger than 100, and I would seek a 'president'—one man—not a 'presidium.' To save money."

23

How large might it be back in his home country of England, where he would now probably be refused entry? Churchman, certainly. Many land owners, also by inheritance. Sometimes an overlap of both of those. Should the entire male population have one vote each? But he did not spend much time on these questions just now. He ignored them and waited.

It was tingling. He waited for more 'inspiration.' It was so necessarily simple, he hated to add anything further.

The Colonies could take such a paragraph, and if the Crown asked what sort of organization the Colonies had, they would reply we have a 'constitution.' We are *this* kind of group, not *that*, etc. With *these* kinds of features, not those.

It was magical to be in the new world with this thought. It was provided by the fact that it was some 3500 miles from London to Philadelphia, and London was not needed to answer every single question that came up.

This, in turn, brought him back to the marvelous sermon, to the Christian's 'new world' in Christ that didn't need to answer to the religious constrictions of Judaism that Paul had grown up within. A 'new creation' Paul had called it. Instead of the rather dismal way of putting things that Judaism had, there was Paul's list of qualities—but not *'rules.'* They were the *fruit* of the Spirit of God working in a person, 'about which you don't make *rules.*' They were personal virtues, attitudes; strong enough to bond together a people.

It seemed to Paine that on this, the Christian message had something supremely sensible, even for those only under the secondary influence of it. There were many other things that he wanted to get rid of.

'Freed *for* freedom.' Paine read the Galatian passage again. Was there anything in this 'recipe' for this 'constitution' where yet another wave of slavery could splash in and erode the 'land'? There was no rule that everyone subscribing would be Christian, but it was certainly modeled on what Christian freedom consisted of. No questionable union of a government with *one* religion, but certainly a place for all of them.

But there was a challenge here which Tom would not realize for some time. In the civic arena—not the quieter confines of Christian churches—he would seek to dismantle 'the plague of the world'—the British empire and its supporting religion—with teeth, with vitriole, with scathing speech. He would attack with an over-the-top style, a *'force de plume'* that would incite the under-represented masses to his side. It would be easily grasped by those drinking in pubs across the English countryside. It wouldn't be virtuous! But the pragmatic question was: would it all go the direction he hoped?

Copies of Paine's booklets would sneak into England and thousands circulated in larger cities. But there were folks in the English countryside who had the harder lot in life. They didn't get the opportunity to learn to read, but they heard someone in a pub or around a dinner table reading a selection of Paine outloud, and the laughter was so raucous, their ribs hurt. They'd walk away from the gathering, holding their sides and wiping tears of laughter from their eyes, remarking "I love *Paine.*" It was possible, for folks like this, that all that Paine was saying could go quite another direction.

He was surprised to find himself sitting with merely one page written down, when he heard the 5 o'clock chime and was hungry. What an afternoon!

2
The Signal

Near Brighton, Sussex, 1798

For years those in England who lived in London had traveled to the south coast vantage points where the bonfires were lit during the attack of the Spanish Armada. There were the beaches and the fantastic views of sheer cliffs. The coastal towns of Sussex had become like resorts, a bit more refined than the shipping centers of Bournemouth and Southhampton to the west. The signal system of bonfires readied the forces on the south coast and dispatched word to London of an attack. Ditchling was the highest point of Sussex, but many other sites were needed for confirmation.

By 1800, the system would be more or less permanent, including some light houses. There were various kinds of signals, including a set of lights for captains to see in storms and know the proximity of dangerous reefs below. The Royal Sovereign Shoals were named for the ship which was snagged there, and many similar reefs required warnings and markers especially in storm season. Various light and sound configurations were used and coded.

In the village of Brighton, a few miles from Ditchling, lived a woman named Millie with an infant now a few weeks old. Lived? It was merely a shed, a hidden back room, while the father weighed their options in their first week of parenting. To that father, the new-born stood for a whole set of tasks he didn't want. Unmarried, Millie relied on meager amounts to arrive from this aggressive, anti-religious fellow, Fitzwilliam Summers. But there was now something else to wait on. Fitz had said to wait for a signal from him.

Fitz was a firebrand, a provocateur. A disciple of Paine, of the French Revolution, of the Johnson circle. Paine had him laughing with his comments about "His *Mad*jesty" and had provided Fitz with a model for speaking to the tradesman, the buyers and sellers, the fisherman of the south coast. He did not have an education and could only read a little, but he had heard several readings of the radical texts. This disciple of Paine had pledged allegiance to "The absurdities of religion must be slain with laughter:"

> Your church must be sensible to your mind. You don't need to shop in the East, or "His Madjesty's" church, or the Papacy, or the Mohammedan church. They all have the same structures, although some are more inviting than others! Forget about revelation from God! What you do, or believe, must make sense for now and today.

A woman cut in. "'Now and today'? You want that we should watch the mating of the deer in the wood, then? That's now and today. It makes sense to them."

Fitz fired back. "And a loveless marriage arranged so 50 acres could be joined to a 100? That makes sense? Women as breeding stock? How can you accept that?

"Now look at Ditchling. The highest point here in the south. It has been 'revealed', you know, that 'if you have faith, you could move that thing.' Now, why would you want to move that? It's nonsense. But I digress. What about all those who have said they have faith to do so? Nothing happens. So what is this 'Christ' all about and how does he get his followers?"

And so he could go on, for quite a spell in the market, but not having any money and not much of a prospect for earning anything, he would retreat to find a writer to take down some original thoughts, unless a foreman seeking some day-labor had come asking.

Other times the crowd threw refuse at him. He had heard whispers of accusations of sedition, but he was invincible enough as a young man not to care. He was naïve about the toll of the French Revolution. Hadn't Paine written whole sections of THE AGE OF REASON to them?

Fitz had his motivation to change England more from his own poor upbringing than from knowing the latest about Paine. Fitz had not even heard of Edward Lennox, a recent son of royalty—the Duchess of Lominster—who was a martyr for revolution by 1798. Edward had studied under Paine over in France during the Reign of Terror, and yet still intended on changing England the same way. It was through Edward that Irish support for some type of revolution was gaining and men were being armed for battle.

The name 'His Mad-jesty' had been earned, of course. In one case, there was a favorite Duke who had died, yet the King continued providing three meals a day for his family 15 years later when no one was there to eat them. There was exceeding competition among the servants to be employed there and enjoy the fine meals the next day.

In another, George IV was apparently unable to absorb the concept of a deficit budget. "Bring me the Royal Treasury books," he roared to his secretary. "I'll show you the money!" The books were brought, and the secretary explained that the bottom lines he was viewing were negative and {bracketed} accordingly. "Nonsense!" blasted the King. "You can't have books like this without money!" His staff had no choice but to agree with the usual "Very well."

>|<

During her 'confinement,' Fitz would sometimes continue campaigning with Millie at the shed. "*Marriage?* There's no reason for it. That novelist I spoke to you about--Jane Evans--is perfectly happy just living with another couple as a third partner, and there's no reason we can't be."

"You mean you're going to find a *third* partner here? What's this about? They better have money! And that novelist uses a man's name to publish! What does that tell you? She doesn't want anyone to know, and the man is getting the best part of the deal! But at least they have money."

"I don't know that they do. Time will change that—about the man's name, I mean. Maybe the money, too. She grew up as an evangelical, then she left it. That's what I've been trying to tell you. Paine says now is the time when reason should break out, and get rid of so many stupid traditions...*superstitions.*"

"Well," Millie fired back, "Speaking of *reasons*: I don't have any money. Not that would raise a child, mind you. There are no orphanages for miles, and I've seen the orphanages in

London. No thanks, no life for a child... Not that this is any better."

As far as Fitz was concerned, the birth had entirely changed Millie, and he couldn't get her to *laugh*, and that used to be the ticket.

"I have a plan and the problem will be over quickly and we'll immediately depart inland past Brighton. I have some contact now with Paine's circles and I see a way to set up a speaking itinerary about the ridiculous way religion is hanging on here."

"And what," asked Millie, "is the career in that? What is our future?"

"There will be a new order; the people will need to be represented."

Millie stared blankly. "There is no money."

All this had been said in a night visit by Summers to the shelves where Millie and the newborn were 'stored' in Brighton.

>|<

It would have been better if Millie had grown up in an orphanage. She was born to a woman from Southhampton and was taken to Brighton by plan in a few years, rather than grow up in the circles in which the mother was stuck near the port's docks. There was more of a chance of working for a decent merchant or trader or fisherman; there was more proper money.

A coachman had told the mother he would give her a free return ride to Southhampton the same day. The mother spent a total of 3 hours on the ground in Brighton with Millie that day, showing her how to find day jobs where there were many more fisherman with fish to peddle and homes to serve than her own circle.

Millie liked her first impressions of Brighton, but she had no idea her mother was hopping back on that coach and disappearing forever.

Millie had always been too busy even as a child working or trying to find work to realize that there were children her age who lived cared-for in families, or sometimes in homes for children. A few years after her realization of that, she began to ask what seemed to others to be the first question: where *was* her mother? Her father?

Then she began to resent all that, and it was in that frame of mind of abandonment and resentment that she heard a young man speaking in the street about the faults of the rich in allowing so much of the population to scrape by and for children to straggle along in life. That young man was Fitz Summers, and he was a disciple of Thomas Paine who intended to fix all that one day in England.

Millie couldn't resist, and at 16, she had blossomed enough that she caught the eye of Fitz. He was no man of means, nor even a place to live, nor any income, but he cared about her and was her first attentive male relationship. He really seemed to have caught on to something that would be a settled life. She barely had time to find anyone in the places where she worked to ask about what happens when you are in love, and when the young man has this overpowering desire to hold you close, to lay with you.

And then she knew everything, and was pregnant.

It was among the shacks of Brighton that Fitz found a place for Millie to keep out of view as he scrambled for day jobs to find them food, or sharpened his petty theft skills. He had no idea what he was doing, but he didn't want to lose his meager contacts with people who might have a secret interest in the radical Mr. Paine just because he had an unmarried woman friend who was showing that she was pregnant. There was no way to get back first impressions. So there he was, out and about, while she was holed up in a tiny corner wishing she could find out what happens next when you are 'carrying a *bairn*'—a baby. She agreed to stay out of view, because she didn't know where any of this was going.

The alley had something of a view of the people walking the street, and she would watch out the peep hole in the wall and if she saw a woman with a big belly out and about, she was going to dash out and talk. She did not realize that in the more refined area where they lived, such women were 'in confinement' and many days went by without any sightings.

Even the birth ended up being haphazard. She had no idea what she was doing, but was fortunate to have had an easy labor. She had hardly any spare rags, and few blankets, and finally Fitz came back, and learned that "it" had happened, and she really needed help--and things--one way or another.

"OK, look, I've got to at least do one thing here, and I need you here with the *bairn*."

"How do you mean?"

"At dusk tonight, I'll feed him—God knows I have plenty of milk!—and then I've just got to go down to the sea and bathe. I need an hour. Actually, I need money for the bath house."

"But what will he do? I don't have money for the bathhouse."

"Sleep. He'll be asleep. Then I need you to go find me some rags. I need rags. He needs rags. Rags, rags, rags."

"At night?"

"I don't know. Maybe someone got lazy with their laundry. You figure it out. Then I need to know what we are doing here, Fitz."

"What about newspaper?"

"What?"

"I could try to read what I need and then crumple them over and over til they are soft."

"You can't read."

"But I see names and I can take them to that friend near the postal office who reads them to me."

"We could try crumpling them, yes. I don't know. Just...don't think about your 'new England' plan or Paine and all that for a week or two, OK?"

But it was a miserable swipe at an insurmountable problem. For several days, he was in and out with no regular success. He'd had to come up with a plan all right, but it was not a plan for money for Millie and the baby. He never even named him. It was a plan to put it all *behind* them.

> | <

Fitz returned one day, and from his eyes, Millie knew it was time for action, but again not quite knowing what. She was to be ready with a box he had found—or kiped—for clothes. No, she wouldn't be packing for the baby. Summers also left a basket with her and told her to feed and wrap up the baby snugly in the basket when the time came. But most important, he set her up with a message.

"I'll be having a boy deliver a message to you as soon as certain conditions are confirmed. Four unmistakable words. When you get it, you go after dark to the sea, and put the basket there."

She gasped. "There. The sea? In a boat? We're not—"

"We are leaving him to the forces of nature, or the acts of God, or whatever they call it. It's our fleece, our rod of Elijah—although they would surely call us Jezebel!"

She massaged her forehead, not quite knowing what she was hearing. "The *four words*? What are the four words?"

"*Storm arriving; tide receding.* When you get that message from me by a boy, you are to leave immediately after dark and walk the basket into the sea and let it float away, then you meet me at the King's Coaches. We will drive through the night. I know a remote farm north of Brighton."

She sobbed. "No, I won't, *I can't*."

"You *will*." and Fitz made toward her in a threatening stance. "It's not as though there are any other options!"

"So...we are not to have any *faith* at all, even...about things like this? I...understand about '*always being in love...*', and, oh, what did your other radical- say, "*and therefore we should never marry...*'but...are we just to live on *passion*?"

"Are you afraid to do so?" he said heatedly, then paused. "That child is not really a person until it has a mind and *reason,* don't you see?... Fine! Then you leave it at the back of church or whatever you want, but no one can see you! And then get yourself to King's Coaches." He got up and left.

His 5 year seniority and that glimpse that he might actually take a swat at her swayed the day. There was something overwhelming about that memory. Clothes could be mended, fences could be rebuilt, but she had been *that* close to a blow to her 17-year-old face that could scar for life, that might never be repaired.

Millie now realized she had nothing at all, truly nothing, but a trip in a coach away from this miserable hole and the hiding and the secrecy, which she half-heartedly decided to take.

It was one thing to think he might plan such a thing in an obscure future, but now it had actual times and meeting places— *and threats!* She wretched. She worked on the skill of feeling nothing. It was a horrible few days. She hid from everyone. She

35

didn't nurse unless there was no other way to keep the child quiet. Then she got angry about being milk-wet all of sudden, and resented it *all*. *She* was going to walk *herself* into the sea!

> | <

The south coast stormwinds had come up, moving crazily about the door of Signaler Abner Pruitt's shack atop Ditchling that night where he had raised a mighty bonfire for warning to vessels at sea. He was nearly ready to shut in from the storm and the dark, until rebuilding later, when he detected movement down below on the shore, a tiny light. Someone was down there, walking into the water.

He put on his coat again and got his lamp and horse mounted and dashed down the escarpment on a trail that now, thanks to months of duty here, was something he could now do in the dark.

When he realized it was a woman, he sunk a bit as he had no skill in talking to someone crazy who was here at such an unlikely time. Especially a *woman*. He had managed the rage and counterattacks of soldiers in hand to hand battle, but to see a young half-angel deliberately dangling so close to this noisy, wind-blasted, devouring mouth, made him undone. And who would be walking into the water right now unless they were beside themselves or suicidal? The light was too poor to make out anything else.

She had pulled her dress up to her knees and was in that deep. "It is better" she whispered as she set the basket upright in the outbound drift of a wave.

Back she came, sloshing away in the various depths of the surf, and when she looked up and saw Abner's light, she shrieked, and covered her face tighter with her scarf. She looked once where the basket was last seen and it was sucked back in to the steep surf, gone forever.

"What are you doing here?" Abner yelled. "This is as mighty a storm as—"

She was young and quick and grabbed the box and ran off.

Abner scanned the water to see if anything else was there but recognized nothing. He turned his attention back to her and noticed as she reached a certain level, there she had a small lamp, she stopped to look one more time, and her head fell back. Her face shown one more time looking back in the light of her lamp.

He looked up on the 200 foot cliff and his fire was out of view. He needed to be sure of it, but wished he could find out what this was all about. He plodded along back up the climb to his position, dreading the fact that he was only making the trail more treacherous with each step. He would check the next morning in daylight.

He would report the irregularity to the Admiralty but find no damage or breach to the lighting system.

>|<

The Bourneboro Home for Children, Brighton
Elnora awoke with a gasp. It was an occupational hazard. At 5 a.m., she would think of something, the strangest thing, that had been missed in the care of the 14 children there at Bourneboro. She really needed to stop doing that; maybe she needed to find something relaxing to take before sleep for it. But she also had to listen for the children. Then she would realize it could be taken

care of today, and then she would realize that this was God's alarm clock, because it was 5 a.m., and she should get started.

She actually slept in the same room with the youngsters and now to warm up a bit, she would light fires and then crawl in with one of the young ones and organize her day in her head, or at least her morning.

Pastor George Holford would be by at some point in the weekday mornings for a short lesson. Hopefully, he would also bring some money for the general budget, but it was day-to-day on that.

The home had been established near Holford's chapel, remodeled from some estate from days gone by.

When there was stirring in the bed next to hers, and a little boy woke up and propped himself up, Elnora looked over and whispered.

"Everything's alright, Tommy. You're still here. You don't have to move house anywhere. Come and climb in if you are cold, but make yourself thin! And hope the bed doesn't collapse!"

One of the goals of the home was that, upon taking in a child, they would be with their siblings and settled there at least 4 years. Many had utterly chaotic times in their lives and still thought each day was going to end horribly. Elnora, on her 6 nights there each week, made a complete round each month, so that they all could start at least one day in bed with 'momma.' Elnora was sunshine in their lives.

>|<

Near Uckfield, The Weald, Sussex

The coach wheeled on through the night in the dimmest of light.

Millie reported coldly. "There was a shiplight—" But Fitz nearly slapped her mouth to stop her. One could not be too careful in these parts. There were three others in the dark coach and who knows if they were asleep or what they might remember.

The carriage creaked along in the night en route to Uckfield and turned north beyond. The driver announced a stoppage and warned all to stay with ear of his cry to re-board if they got out.

At the stopover, Fitz grabbed Millie and took her away from the pub and stable there.

"*What lightman?*"

"I just came back from the waves and there he was. He must have run all the way down from the top, thinking I was in danger or something."

Summers turned to face her, to pick up any clue from her face.

"What do you think he saw?"

"I don't know...I screamed when I saw him. I guess there's guilty screams, I don't know. He said it was very dangerous or something. I didn't stop or anything."

Summers calculated. *The Admiralty. They'll be wanting to know if there was any plot or plan to disrupt the light system.*

"And then what happened?"

"I don't know. I left, into town, to the coachhouse. He went back up, I reckon."

"But still. You screamed. He'll be down there in daylight and there'll be others from the Admiralty, to see what mischief was brewing. Damn."

"I need a drink. Oh, now my milk is coming. I need rags. I need my box."

"What? The driver won't get it... Why didn't you think of that?"

39

Fitz moved through the pub quickly, asking the host for a knapkin to mop up for a friend. He got out his knife and ran back to Millie, hurriedly dividing the knapkin in halves for her, and she put them to use.

>|<

The next morning they had only been awake at Slickson's Farm for an hour, and she had met some of the ladies there, mostly permanent workers, when she went to find her box, and talk to Fitz. She found a note.

> *I'll be gone a week at least. I have business back in Brighton I could not finish then. Our hosts have said there is some work for you for your daily keep.*
> *--Fitz*

She was mystified. This person, this kind of life, was going to take some getting used to. Just as she thought they were working their way to London, bang—he was gone the other direction. He didn't have money—until he did. It was hard for her to think of herself as a partner in all this.

>|<

Another project of Pastor Holford's was participation on the Tilson estate housing. One of the estates of this evangelical member of the House of Lords had been redesigned on principles that would make any modern planner proud of the project. An acreage of the estate which contained some farmable land had been selected and then the layout of it called 'emparking' was surveyed and measured and marked.

On the Tilson Park Estate, the designers had kept all new construction around the perimeter. This resulted, for one thing, in a perimeter road. Home plots were then laid out on both sides of the road, the outside half being built up against the existing boundary lane of the property, and the inner half having the open farmable land on the back beyond its gardens. Each home would have a garden.

The farmable land was then preserved as much as possible, with the following exceptions: a pond was preserved and the area immediately around this natural feature was to become a park in the modern sense. And alongside this there was to be an open sporting field preserved. Otherwise the 'emparkment' landscape would look just as it always had, and preserve the fields as much as possible for production and openness.

The financial direction of Lord Tilson took another clever direction. Brighton was full of capable workers but obsolete housing. He researched the optimum size of building crew and learned that groups of 8 were ideal for the builder-managers of such crews to use efficiently.

Tilson then fronted the construction material money for 8 homes, one for each family represented on a crew, to proceed on a round-robin of construction, repeating each phase 8 times, until 8 homes were completed together, ending with a loan of materials to be paid off without interest. The families could eventually sell if that amount could be paid back out of the sale, but most families were far too much in need of the stability of a nice, new home and chose to stay and make the material payment.

The notion that no interest would be charged was a huge statement. Many had read the line by Paine that "If you talk to a London merchant about Scripture, they think you meant '*scrip*' and they will tell you how much that is worth at the Stock

Exchange. Ask them about theology, and they will say they know no such person—no one by the name Theo--at the 'Change..." So in an economy that competed for as much interest as possible, the evangelical plan at Tilson's had taken an astoundingly charitable stance. And the plan of the Tilson family was to simply repeat the process when the first set of 8 were complete.

The workers would be qualified for a home not only on skills but also on the length of time spent in dismal housing, and on the ability of the rest of the family to sponsor them. It wasn't a perfect plan, but it was inspiring and was a more worthwhile prospect than anything else they had at the time.

The homes were in rows with joining walls, with flower plantings in front and vegetable gardens in the back.

When one cycle of 8 was completed, another was started. Some of the participants began professions of their own. Matthew Woodland became a foreman of the next cycle of building at age 19, and then worked independently once the 2nd cycle—and 16 homes—were completed through his efforts.

Then there were the delicate cases involving both projects—the orphanage and the housing--that Holford needed to coordinate. For example, a group of three children arrived from Bournemouth because the father had died at sea. The mother was working but it was not enough to keep the family. But there was a single man at work at the homes at Tilson's who had met her at a church and declared intentions to provide for them once the home was ready. It was going to be one of the happier outcomes of both efforts.

>|<

Summers lurked around Brighton's pubs again, keeping to himself, waiting for any bits of information that might come through about what had happened. Most of all, seeing if the incident of the woman in the storm surf came up.

Then, in a few days, there was word of an approaching storm again from someone in contact with Beachy Head. As dusk approached, he made his way out there and until the storm light system was up. He wasn't going to make an incident before the light was burning.

When he was sure he had his man, and the fellow had not retired for the first watch, he wandered nearby the shack in his best imitation of being drunk. The lightman, with his fine Admiralty luminary, was concerned about what a person was doing up there at the cliff at that time of the night, and whether he would like a pointer about the way back. Instead, Summers slid closer to the edge of the 250 foot shear.

"The 'way back'! What would I d—d—do with the way back? Ha, ha, ha!"

"Come on, mate, don't be daft. You'll be soaked soon and—"

The proximity to the edge gave Summers his moment, but he was too busy with his act to ask the fellow if he was there for the last storm. Summers feigned a stumble by the edge and grabbed the lightman's arm awkwardly sending him to his death below, the lamp bouncing along the edge, and Summers on his back. He was almost surprised the plan had worked so well and reached for the lamp to right it.

He listened through the howls and shone the lamp over the edge to see if anything was snagged, but how could it be with such an abrupt edge and shear face?

He stepped into the shack and looked around. A little food, a quality timepiece from the Admiralty for when the lightman would have awakened, and rebuilt the fire. Summers' head was pounding now, trying to think clearly about the

'scenario.' *What would it look like if the fellow just slipped?*
Where should the lamp be left? And a hundred other questions.

And then he realized the best thing he could do—and perfectly safe—would be to wait there and rebuild it in 4 hours at midnight, and then the 'mishap' would appear to have occurred after midnight. He charged back out into the weather and checked the fuel supply. Something about this made him relax. He yawned at it all and went into the bunk.

200 feet below, Lightman Benjamin Carstens' body was awkwardly strewn above the beach.

> | <

Summers awoke in an hour and looked through the Admiralty records as he made the long wait for the clock to reach the midnight watch. He tried to doze again, but he didn't want to be too far off his timing.

He could follow the dates of the record book, but he wasn't sure about the codes for the weather. For example, there were these entries:

Nov.3	*Twilight*	*AP*
Nov.4	*Midnight*	*AP*
	First light	*AP*
	Midday	*BC*
	Twilight	*BC*
Nov.5	*Midnight*	*BC*

And so on, but he had looked at the front and back of the volume in vain to learn what that meant—if he could read it.

When the midnight rebuilding of the fire was done, he put the lamp out and tossed it whimsically near the edge and took a smaller lamp to get part way down the hill, and back to Brighton. After a late morning nap or two and some breakfast, he would find his way to the London road out of Brighton, and turn toward Uckfield.

3
'Slaughtering Religion'

Slickson's Farm, near Uckfield, Sussex

One evening after dinner, two couples had been invited by the hosts to hear more of what Summers had to say about the new world of reason.

"I'm not saying there is no God. I'm saying that we've all had enough of the corruption and money-changing that goes on in the name of religion—that's why they are all so similar. In order for there to be a revolution in our political lives, there needs to be a revolution about church as well. And about *revelation*."

"The Biblical book *Revelation*?" posed a listener.

"No, but that book has had more than enough time on the stage, and who knows what it means? What I mean is the friction generated among people and between redundant religions through their claims of God-given revealed, *written* truth. Mr. Paine speaks about 'redundancies' quite a bit. And after all their arguing, the churches forget to ask if they need any of it."

"So God is there, but He can't speak. Hmmm."

"You're going to say that the alternative which I bring you is worse."

"What is it?"

47

"*Reason*! It must be reasonable, for us, for now. Look, yes: God exists; yes, if you like, He can speak and bequeath an official book; call it a 'testament' if you will. But when the audience is dramatically different in another time period, can't you agree that there must be ways that God will speak which may have surprising impact on a 'testament'?"

"Yes, something like that."

"But this is where reason comes in. Now look what we've got to let go of, for example, that devil hauling Christ up to a high point like Ditchling and showing him kingdoms. Why didn't he show him America? And were they *both* in it for kingdoms? Then what advantage is Christ? And then there is the devil back there in that garden where evil invaded, so it says. Isn't it time to just have a big laugh about all that?"

"How *could* he have done that back then--was there an America back then?" replied one of the husbands over his drink.

"That's not... I don't mean that, I mean the whole of it is too much of a fantasy and not very interesting. You see, I rather like Christ, alright? But all these strange tales and incidents! He could have just made a sensible statement about not seeking such power, but instead we've got this fabulous story no one knows is true, and which the masses love to mimic and jabber about, generating all their own miracles, until anything sensible that was there is lost.

"His spokesperson Paul says 'Honor the king.' Yet what if that leader is insane, and what if the same Paul said to be as self-governing as possible? How come 'His Mad-jesty' doesn't mention the self-governing part? It's time to laugh, I say!"

"In the meanwhile, look at us here on earth. People preaching that we are fixed in our states of rich and poor. Since creation! And the clergy--how did they manage it so that *they* became as rich as the landed?"

"As rich as?—you mean, they *are* the landed."

"Yes, you're right. That's why the committee across the Channel confiscated all church property, including the Notre Dame. Is there a reason why the church has all these people so occupied with the next life? To ignore this life, and this financial arrangement? You must have heard of Hebert by now.

"And I haven't even begun talking about the Old Testament yet. Of course, I appreciate the sacrificing redeemer of the New Testament. But did the God of the Old Testament really not know how much evil was modeled in the taking of the land of the Canaanites?

"This is why I must agree with Mr. Paine: that the Bible is the poorest-read best-selling book."

Fitz could continue on like this for hours, sounding like these were the questions that stopped everything on the spot.

>|<

Pastor George Holford had been reading in Josephus' THE JEWISH WAR for some time now, and he was stumped. His mentor had been a professor in Plymouth, Dr. Halworth, and he hoped his son would sit under the same instructor. But Holford was not stumped by that. And he had heard some second-hand comments about a young speaker named Summers which had wowed audiences at pubs and so-forth though Fitz himself was said to be in hiding. "Hiding" in those days meant you might sleep in a barn out in Henfield, or if you really wanted to be safe, you'd go out to Uckfield.

No, Holford was puzzled at his research in THE JEWISH WAR account to find that Josephus was a priest and reader, and mentioned a prophetic revolt that would ruin the country. That would be found in Daniel 8, and would led by an engaging character. The movement was first called 'the rebellion that desolates' there; the text got right to the point.

What amazed Holford was that here he was in the stormy times of England about 1800, where a sizable portion of the population thought the king crazy. And where the independent Americans had sent a 'missionary' of freedom back to Europe to help revolution break out against all aristocracy.

Yet at just this time Holford had landed up on a document that historians would one day call the most complete account of a cataclysm in antiquity. And in the center of it was a rebellion that would be vastly outnumbered yet try against hope to seize freedom for Israel.

And now, he had found, the author of the account *knew* failure was expected!

Holford decided it was time to send a letter to the sagacious Dr. Halworth over in Plymouth.

To the esteemed Dr. Halworth,

I recall fondly our many discussions of theological questions as you brought me up to the level of explanation that is needed in our times. It certainly paid off.

So it is obviously to you that I must turn with this question: what are we to make of Josephus' knowing of a colossal failure of a rebellion from the prophets' writings? Was this always in the back of his mind?

And being a priest as well as a captain who deserted Israel's meager forces, was he of the same mind of that Caiaphas-- who was moved to prophesy during Christ's work that 'it would be better if one person died, than for the entire country to perish' (Jn 11:50 etc). So he

*was one of the few who <u>truly</u> did know that the gift of
Christ was for all who believe from all nations.*

*Yet he also struggles to pre-empt the country
from grief and destruction if possible. Even though 'it was
written.'*

*I am certainly aware that we cannot explore every
question that might arise from the record, but if anyone
would have thought about these things, it would be you.*

*In the service of the kingdom,
Pastor George Holford
Brighton, Sussex*

>|<

Millie would listen to the best of answers by Fitz; she had
memorized many of them, but it was difficult for Millie now. Fitz
could put out for hours, but they had no money, and no
prospects.

Then she was wet again, and her heart was scattered all
over the place trying see how the raising—or now the loss—of a
child was to be a totally *rational* thing. She groaned and sighed
and wept. She wasn't keeping up how she looked. The other
women had not yet connected with her about this, or were afraid
to ask the obvious about the wet clothes Millie was dealing with
every few hours.

Every day—every hour—Millie would face this dilemma
with Fitz. Is all this fuss about truth or not? Was she
sophisticated enough or not?

She finally managed to eek out an answer to other ladies
during washing: their child had died after a few weeks. No

surprise about that. They were never in a proper home, no family around. It was not a marriage; they kept to themselves.

"So this belief—he says children don't really matter until they show some ability to think and reason—it became true in your case on very harsh terms."

Millie collapsed disconsolate. "It was the height of life and the dregs all in one year. Before I showed, I would go out and look at the cliffs. The land at its height and then one step later it's the bottom. I never thought that would be the picture of my life."

"You sorry thing. How did you meet this man, this Mr. Summers?"

"Laughter. I'd never laughed before in my life until I heard him. I'd never heard irreverence until him. I mean, he was just trying to pry away all the barnacles, you know. All the barnacles covering the rock, so we can get down to the rock. 'Religion must be slaughtered by laughter.' But now—now it's turned dangerous. Now what he says about children--" (she had to catch her tongue) "he's starting to...sound like the French..." And she choked and stopped herself. "The people don't even have names in public; it's just *Citizen*. At least prisoners get numbers..."

The other women had stopped their work, too, trying to figure out what to say.

"So will you marry? Has he declared his intentions?"

Millie couldn't see through her tears and folded up in discomfort. She was holding her tummy, and concerned that something really was wrong inside after all.

One of them spoke out. "Millie, I know you've just left Brighton, but I know someone there. You should go see her."

"Brighton?" Millie scoffed. "But that would mean..."

52

"I know, I know. He'll just have to deal with it. We've got to take care of you, child. Now, let's make some plans."

>|<

At another discussion evening with Summers, a visitor had objected. "I don't think you've quite understood what Tom Paine means about atheism. He has some agreement with Mr. Robespierre, you know. He knows the favorite accusation about the republic is that it is irreligious, and barbaric."

Millie was listening and that was quite enough. There was now a contradiction about Fitz. Either he hadn't done his homework, or he knew and was intending to procede that way.

"It's destructive to *civility!*" the visitor spoke even louder. "That's what I mean. Atheism is authoritarian. When public speech turns vulgar and bitter, the masses will turn to the unthinkable and violent. We only need to look across the channel."

Millie avoided looking at Summers at the meeting. But he looked at her. He used to get some validation there, but it was fading.

>|<

"Look, Millie, I just want you to know a line that I know is from the apostle Paul. I was looking forward so much to our third child. 'Rounding out the family' I thought. 'There won't be one child vs. the other. There'll be three and they will have a little mate to cherish and look after when I get to the point where I've had too much to do at the end of the day.'

"But it didn't happen that way. The labor started, but I could tell." Kathryn teared up. "Something was wrong. There just wasn't any movement and you thought you could remember the last movement, but I couldn't, so I didn't know what to tell the doctor and the midwife.

"All I knew was now no one knew what to say. The midwife was stroking my face as I realized there was no life. My husband was stunned. And then after a day, I was laying there trying to regroup and I started calling. My friend was concerned that something else had happened, but I needed my two kids badly, and I couldn't believe how beautiful they looked and how tightly I pressed them against me.

"And then, it was kind of over. I could walk and everyone was alright, and I had my strength, although my doctor kept me in the house with my feet up half the time.

"And now look—there's four!"

Millie reflected as they walked around a field and made checks on various animals. "A line. You mentioned a line."

"*He comforts us in all our troubles, so that we can comfort those in any trouble with the comfort we ourselves have received from God.* You see, it's meant to strengthen others, not to increase hopelessness."

"Hmmm. I'll get there, I think. But I don't know how."

"I know, but in a way, that's the fun part. The surprises. God will help you, and although your Fitz came here to seek safety, you may have been brought here for very different reasons."

Millie smiled slightly when she heard that.

"I have a letter ready to someone I know who will try to work out a situation and help you get there."

"What happened in your case—what was the surprise?"

Kathryn chuckled. "At first there were some clouds of grief and I thought 'I will never love my husband as much as before' or 'I will regret that my children are missing that one and nothing will be the same.' But all that went away, and I had this enormous desire for my husband, and eagerly became pregnant again. And then I decided to add a line to the marker of the lost one: 'Taken by surprise.' Because there is more than one path there."

> | <

Paine's book lay on the table between Pastor George Holford and Miles Everton at The Pig and Pie pub in Brighton. Holford nodded at the book.

"Never mind the fact that it is illegal to handle such a thing in England, let's discuss where we are doctrinally. What things would you define as superstition?"

Miles continued. "Who wouldn't have trouble with a talking snake? And what was it about that tree that was so impermissible? But then, is that the point? Or is it just there to say that a line was crossed—a war declared—and evil has spread ever since?"

Holford countered. "And if we go along with the Deists of the recent past, we end up with an account that has no roots in the past, or has roots in events that *never happened*. What good is that? This idea that it would all be better if it was unproven, if it was *removed* from the realm of proof—where does that come from?"

The reader replied uneasily. "Aye, I see what you mean. So, this Mr. Paine—has he challenged events that happened or has he said the same as you?"

"He claims the Bible to be poorly read, yet best-selling. No, we have not had a direct exchange yet."

"Yes, poorly-read. Yet at other times he—Paine--reads very well: '*Rich and poor are not places fixed by God, but male and female are.*'"

Holford straightened up. "Indeed! Can you imagine someone tinkering with *that* difference as though it were a toy!"

"No, I cannot."

"And look at the design of creatures, of the human body. Just the hand. How amazing that we have such a tool at our disposal. So, I say, when you consider the alternatives, I come down to the Creator as described in those pages."

"I agree. Have you found *anything* that you can agree with Mr. Paine about?"

Holford pondered. "He has said there is a God and that humans have added on 'redundancies' of various associated beliefs. I accept that. But I will tell you what my concern is, though it may surprise you. He has abandoned *manners*."

Miles was stumped at this. "*Manners*?"

"Paine lets himself slide into vulgarity and graphic expressions for effect. But I don't think he *understands* the effect. You see, when he wants to criticize a movement for its *policies* that are crude and violent, he will lose his way. The Revolution did. It's one thing to imprison a leader for mishandling public money. It's quite another barbaric thing to put a princess's head on a pike and parade it through the streets of Paris."

"Shall we meet again next week?"

"Aye. It is a very necessary conversation."

They shook hands.

> | <

Martin Holford's birthday celebration would also celebrate two years of ministry studies in Plymouth, under evangelical Professor

Halworth. Part of the reason for returning home to Brighton was for Martin to consult with his father about his own next role in ministry, and how much further study was truly needed.

Another reason was that correspondence with a young lady in connection with his father's church had sweetened. Elnora Picking had been found to have a natural gift managing at the orphanage. She was 'Momma' to the 14 stragglers at the Bourneboro estate home, now an orphanage ministry of Holford's Brighton Evangelical Church.

Elnora and Matthew had known each other as children. And were now corresponding. Matthew informed her that he would also be asking his father if he could propose an engagement. The Pickings had attended the church soon after it formed and Matthew could see no objection, other than the specific questions of having a living. What, for example, does the son of an established pastor do about that, and where? Was there room at Bourneboro or would Elnora prefer not to live her newlywed life there at the orphanage?

All these questions and more were swirling around Elnora and Martin at the birthday celebration, and at the smallish ball that Mrs. Holford had arranged—4 chamber musicians and mostly church friends, a few older children from the orphanage dressed up, and a few of the builders from this cycle of the construction works going on nearby at the Tilson Estate.

As affairs went for the Holfords, it was very grand, only a step down from a wedding reception. There was tasty finger food, and cakes.

The chamber band played Martin's favorite song, "We're Marching To Zion" and the crowd filled it out boisterously. Since it was a party, not a worship service, they 'marched' around on the choruses:

Come we that love the Lord
And let our joys be known;
Join in a song with sweet accord,
And thus surround the throne.

We're marching to Zion
Beautiful, beautiful Zion
We're marching onward to Zion
The beautiful city of God.

Then there was the "So Say All of Us" when they were about to cut the birthday cake. And a verse from "God Save the King."

God save our gracious king! Long live our noble king!
God save the king!
Send him victorious, Happy and glorious,
Long to reign over us;
God save the king!

Martin made his father proud by following those lines with: *"Give to Caesar what is Caesars, and to God what is God's."* And all those present applauded.

The last visitor left at midnight.
Except Millie.

4
'He···Might···Be···Here'

Millie "made it" to the party, but not as an official visitor; she found a dark porch across the street from the Holford's and waited and watched in the cold. At the end of the evening, a handsome couple walked a few blocks away to the Bourneboro home, and Millie knew it must be her. She followed carefully.

The young man kissed the hand of the young lady, and she disappeared within. He returned the way he came. Millie tracked all this from the shadows.

She had arrived back in Brighton on a fish wagon that had delivered near Uckfield. She had to cover her face from the odor with one hand, and hold the sideboards with the other. But she was there, and it was dark. She had some directions, landmarks from the woman back in Uckfield who would preserve her secret. Fitz would guess her location to be anywhere but Brighton with all the commissioned investigating going on by the Admiralty to figure out the death of Carstens.

And now after the exhaustion of travel, the sore back and neck muscles and bottom, the relief of fresher air, and the adrenaline for the final approach to reach the Holford's, she was delirious at best, and about to collapse. Everything was strained, and everything depended on the next moment.

Martin was now gone out of view. Millie saw some light in the orphanage, and waited til all was dark. And then the unexpected happened. She was curled up as small as she could make herself, and in as much dark as she could find, with an eye on the front door of Bourneboro, when she fell asleep in that position.

When she awoke, she cried, for she now had no idea how much time had passed, and she had wanted to knock and speak to the young lady while all was dark, but before she had fallen asleep. But her limbs were aching and lifeless and she just had to stretch out. It was raining. She was getting wet.

It was all she could do to make it to the front door, where she collapsed in a thud against the door, rain dousing her face, turned down hopelessly.

> | <

At about 2 am the night of the birthday party, Elnora was awakened by a 'thud' at the front door and threw on a robe. She unbolted the front door, and when she lifted the latch, she could tell that something was leaning hard into the door.

It was a rain-soaked young woman, shivering and delirious. Elnora quickly dragged her in far enough to close the door from the rude weather, and ran upstairs to the oldest girl's bed. She woke her from her sleep and guided her down as quiet as possible, and they then managed to get Millie on to a couch and somewhat dried, and covered with extra blankets. Fires were out but Elnora chose the kitchen fire over the front room to get tea prepared for this pitiful creature. Then she took the girl back to her bed and with a quick backrub, she had her settled.

There weren't introductions or explanations just yet. Actually, Millie's first weak words were "He... might... be... here..." This meant nothing to Elnora, except she was glad to have at least some means of communication.

Elnora didn't ask anything yet, just continued to mop up. There were no wounds or bleeding or injuries that she could see or detect. Just the exposure of the weather.

The tea was finally ready and Elnora added milk and a bit of sugar. There was some light, finally, in Millie's eyes.

"Miss...Holford?" she said roughly.

"*Eventually* Holford," Elnora smiled proudly. "I think he will speak to my father this week."

"Then...who...are you?"

"Elnora. Picking. This is the Bourneboro Home."

"I'm to find Mrs. Holford...in some connection to this home..." And now there was some presence in Millie's eyes, and she reached for a coat pocket. "I have a letter about me...for her...from a woman who sent me here from the country."

"The country?"

"The farms. We were at a farm...not enough work...and my...boyfriend...has to stay low..."

"To stay low?"

"He believes we need the thoughts of Paine here in England...but it's banned you know, they are banned. So we don't have money, but please, miss, you won't put me out for what I say next."

"You don't seem to be a French spy! No, I don't suppose I would put you out, but how do you mean?"

"I will tell you first and then I will give you the letter."

Millie dragged through the pathetic facts of the newborn up to this point, the Admiralty man, the wet clothing, the reason she felt compelled to leave her young man, and to come back to find an orphanage in Brighton.

Elnora was the embodiment of compassion, and as she had done with so many of the children here at Bourneboro, she crawled under the blankets with Millie and pulled her close to warm her up even further. They cried together at Millie's predicament.

"Oh..." recalled Millie after there were no more tears. She had put the letter back in the pocket during the retelling. "The letter." Elnora sat nearby again to use the lamp.

To the Holfords,

You may not recall my visit to your church some months ago. But I was impressed with the conversation I had with Mrs. Holford and Elnora Picking. I learned how it was that Pastor Holford had come by the offer from the Bourneboros to put a house to use for the plight of many children in the area, and the good heart of Elnora.

My friend Millie is in a terrible predicament and I hope you can help her. I think she may need some time to recover, but then she should be of great value to your children as she has brushed so close to abandonment herself.

Her young man was an impractical dreamer, and a hothead thanks to Tom Paine. I am not sure just yet why it is, but I know the last place he would ever look again for Millie is Brighton because some contact turned sour there. He is in no position to be a father or husband.

I hope that you will come to see that Millie was forced into one of two awful choices as he wanted nothing to interfere with his revolution of England. In her youth, she could not see what might happen, nor know her rightful position, nor know how to protect herself from such a person.

Please accept her and restore her to life as best as possible.

> *Yours in earnest,*
> *Kathryn Merrimount*

"I cannot say I recall your friend, but we will give it thought and prayer and do what we can. And yes, I can see where you could be of help here. I think people like him will need to make themselves scarce, from what I've heard. So I think you will be safe here."

But it made no difference. Millie had fallen deeply to sleep.

Elnora scribbled a note to Millie, and placed it on the chair by her couch for Millie to find if she woke up, and returned to bed, hoping for at least another hour of sleep. That line "He might be here" came back to her and she tried to push it away. But that is not a good idea when you are trying to sleep, and she stopped doing that.

>|<

Everton resumed the conversation with the book in plain view on the table again between himself and Pastor Holford. Holford cautiously covered it with his hat to avoid suspicion. "So you, minister of the Gospel, what will be your answer to this problem you mentioned—*incivility* in public discussion of the future of English government?"

"Well, let's broaden this out. Let's not just refer to the matters of a future government, but all of our public discussion. In the case of the New Testament background and message, I set forth the evidence, of course, delivered in elevating speech. I hope that is a model for all exchanges. And questions and answers afterwards, conducted politely. I am not afraid of questions. I do not have to shut you down.

"We also have, as you may know, the Evangelical Alliance to Abolish Vice. You know we are not seeking to close pubs, as you can see; *here* I am. More to the point: here we are, the two of us, in opposition, but we are not shouting or throwing punches at each other.

"But there are excesses right and left. Families abandoned for drink. Women sold as properties in contracts called 'marriages.' Gambling using the precious assets of a family. A political party that believes it must spread by force because its committee knows best—that is also 'vice.' How do these things develop? Why do people do their worst in the worst form possible? So yes, we have said that book is just as much a ruin of society as those other things I mentioned.

"That is why I talk about 'manners' regarding Mr. Paine. You know what's going on. He wants to shock and delight and infect the masses with laughter, yet it will turn careless—mark my words.

"But I have something, my friend, which even a Thomas Paine cannot answer when it comes to *evidence* for Christ. No, not evidence for a certain politic, although there is a sharp angle that falls upon the question of mob rebellion. Even Thomas Paine will not be able to put this in his box of 'redundancies.'"

"And may I know what you are referring to?"

"Soon you will see. I will be back—even here, to this very pub, inviting one and all to hear me. I think the material is so astounding that it needs to be heard across our country, and I intend to do so, in as many kinds of places as possible, even a *Pig and Pie*. Soon you will see. I will invite you personally."

Everton reflected. "I think those people who dismiss proof are perhaps tired of it all sounding like judicial proceedings. They want to know if God *cares*. You could just teach that God cares for people—with your orphanage and your 'commitment' meetings for those who drink, etc."

"Well, look at it this way. Put that we 'believe' taking care of orphans is very important—but never actually have an orphanage. Put that we 'believe' in telling a group of colleagues that you committed that you won't drink—but the group never meets."

"That would get stuck, like a coach of broken wheels."

> | <

Inspired by talks with Miles Everton and others, Holford assembled a publication and presentation on how Christ's divinity is demonstrated in terms that surpass all the miracles about which people doubt: his claim that Jerusalem would be ruined in that generation. From location to location around England, Holford would also transport a sketch study of a painting from the late 1700s with him that depicted the calamitous events as Jerusalem was destroyed.

The sketch or study was a 'mural' 4 foot high and 6 foot wide. Holford had to find a wagon, and as he would drive along through the country, people in the fields would ask about the strange thin package under wraps. Sometimes he would stop right there, unwrap it, and begin teaching.

Above the tumultuous scenes of Jerusalem in flames, up in the heavens, was a portrayal of a bit of organization of the New Testament. The three apostles who spoke of these events and the apostle Paul are shown hovering from clouds and reading from their texts, hoping their voices will be heard by those below.

Holford's assistant was sent around in advance to put up several posters, such as:

THE DESTRUCTION OF JERUSALEM
An irresistible defense of Christ as God and Lord
Pastor George P. Holford
Of Brighton
Sunday Oct 21st, 4 pm
Henfield Anglican Meeting Hall

There was usually no problem filling a hall or meeting space. Holford's remarks would begin with something like this, also found in his brochure:

The raw materials here are Jesus' answers to the disciples about the 'end of the age,' Josephus' accounts, and Eusebius' account. In the correlation of these materials, we find an astonishing development in 1st century Judea.

The Christians appealed first to their Jewish countrymen to become ministers of the Gospel around the world, with some divine help in the event of Pentecost. Further, this appeal was also a warning to that generation, about pursuing its own kingdom and independence too seriously. The warning was it would be

66

taking on an opposing army against which it had very little chance of succeeding.

The leaders of the rebellion became more insolent and suspicious and ruthless as each day went by. The overall situation became more ridiculous. They believed they had a direct connection to the God of Moses who would manifest and defeat the enemy. Some of them claimed the angels who transmitted their Law would themselves reappear as warriors. It has been said that they destroyed themselves.

The predictions by Christ about what would happen are perhaps without parallel for two reasons. First, they were given about 40 years before the events took place. In addition, they speak of things that no one can consider to be merely 'sacred' or 'religious'; they are purely matters of mainstream history at the time, and now of archeology.

What is more, Josephus reluctantly relates some supernatural elements to his Roman superiors about what happened. Had it not been for the quality of witnesses and reports of them, he would have deleted them. But they are forever in the record.

Thus we may say that the closing scenes of the New Testament—the last picture we have of Christ as far as what He did on earth—are perhaps the most solid basis of belief. They are the clearest things that support His divine origin and work that could have been left with mankind to consider.

They are also a warning that if a revolution does not have a Christian basis, it will be worshipped in its own right and stray madly from a sensible center of belief. We British need no reminder of that!

It was then typical for the host of Pastor Holford to take questions from the audience.

> *"What do you mean to say, then, about the place of the Jewish people?"*

None other than the apostles' desire that they be ministers of the same good news of Christ that we aspire to be. The apostles were neither for nor against the nation; they were for the kingdom of God and its mission.

> *"What do you make of the recent attacks on the Bible by deist thinkers and Thomas Paine?"*

I believe that this material settles once for all that there is no question that the unusual events of Christ—miracles, claims—are truly historic. But there was an audience intended for all that. It was *that* decisive generation. They may not all have the same effect on us, for example, the withering of an olive tree. But background about it will eventually bring us a valuable lesson.

> *"What does all this mean for our own constitutional questions here in England?"*

Ah, certainly there is a political implication here about hotheads and about incivility. On these I find Mr. Paine to be an insufferable failure. I know he was inspired by a sermon about Galatians 5. We are moving intelligently toward a *constitutional* monarchy with checks and balances, and foresee the day when all males may vote here as well as in the America which Mr. Paine envisions. I see no need to be a reactionary as Mr. Paine is—unless I were living 3500 miles away where conversations with your leaders take 4 months each turn!

But I do ask you: if you want to accomplish business effectively and inexpensively, would you ask those without money or business experience? I would not, nor have I ever heard of it. Successful plans are made by consulting the wise.

Tea and cakes were then served and the meeting's formality dropped off into various conversations.

Over time, it was a huge boost to Pastor Holford when the law office of Erskine and Kyd, Esquires, validated his material. These attorneys had earlier represented Hardwick, a publisher of Paine, in an effort to preserve freedom of speech. They were now to represent the Crown *against* a publisher, Thomas Williams, who was charged and held for publishing Paine's AGE OF REASON. This book poked satirically at any crack it could in the Biblical account, and at the belief that the classes were ordained since creation, and at the dubious theology of the divine origin of monarchs.

Paine's book was not 'theology;' it was often quoted in the pubs of the country. Yet its posture had a fatal theological flaw in it, and Holford had capitalized on that. Holford had shown the New Testament to be far more grounded in fact than most had imagined, and Erskine could see no useful purpose to all of Paine's vitriole and tearing-down. The Crown won the day. And in addition to this defeat, and to Paine's misunderstanding the English view of the American revolution, and to Paine's second round of trouble in France, it was nearly three decades before any interest in Paine resumed in England.

Fitz was puzzled. He had gone back to Ditchling to detect any details that he could and then returned to Uckfield and those friends to see if they had heard anything.

"She's gone," reported one of the women. "No one seems to know a thing about her. She had no money. You know that."

"I'm afraid in her state of mind that she's in a ditch out here among the fields. How aweful."

"Maybe it's best you don't know."

"And best she doesn't know some things about me."

"Like what?"

"Can't say, can't say. What work is there today? I should be at work."

Everton came again to meet Holford at one of Brighton's beach walks. Holford was surprised he had not been found out by the authorities. This time Everton did not bring a copy of Paine. He had things to ask Holford about where all this was going.

"Aren't you afraid of what is going to happen?"

"How do you mean? That there will be a widespread, volatile revolution in England?"

Holford disclosed: "Well, we may lose this battle, I don't know. But I mean what is going to happen to your faith? Things are happening that will undo it all. Science is going to change everything. And I don't know if you can see this, but even if Paine fails in both England and France, he has somehow made the state very large in both cases—as big as a god.

"Even though Jesus himself asked if he would find faith on earth—or find *the* faith—when he returned, it makes no difference to me. My task is clear. I must present the clearest proof that he was true in all departments. Working backwards through time then, he must have been true about David, about Noah, about Creation.

"You see, science is going to come along and say the only thing that is real are those processes we see going on right now. They'll even say God must be confined to some kind of experiment over at a university and if he is not "there"—on the table, in the dish--then forget it. And thousands of incidents down through history and many cultures are to be dismissed.

"I even suppose some teacher will come along and say, 'Now look at this process. It took 1000 years to accumulate that inch of soil there, or what have you, and so they will simply use mathematical computations to determine everything.

"So yes, I'm afraid of that happening, and that Mr. Paine's 'troops of philosophers' will effect more damage than an invasion from across the Channel—if he ever tries that. But about your own personal safety, I notice you don't have the book this time. I will keep our conversations as confidential, but there is no telling what eyes and ears are in our surroundings. In other words, Miles, I'm asking you your question: aren't *you* afraid?"

>|<

Secularism was a new concept for France, England and America. There could only be experiments.

The experiment in France had not gone very well. In fact, it may have missed the point. Wasn't there a Goddess of Reason—enacted in a parade by one of Paris' female opera celebrities--placed where Notre Dame cathedral had been renamed the Temple of Reason? Why a *goddess*? Why was there a religious way to announce the abolition of religion?

Then down at the very lowest level, there was the 'policing' of the poor. Not helping them, but insisting that they could no longer sit in public crying *'For the love of God.'* That was forbidden. Now they must say *'For the Nation.'* Not that it improved things for them. But the gentleman over in the south English pub had been correct: *'Atheism is dictatorial.'* It always has time for minutia such as the issue of the wearing of a crucifix as a jewelry item or how the poor may speak when begging.

>|<

The Robespierre Reign of Terror was the most irregular sort of reign with absolute power. Inspired by Paine, it also imprisoned *him* from 1793-94. When he appealed for help from his American pals, there was confusion in Washington—the general--because of the fact that Paine had created this structure to begin with. Robespierre was defeated, and his *Committee for National Security* was replaced by the Directory. Although Paine praised the Constitution of 1795 and the three-member Directory—the very *presidium* he had in mind 20 years earlier-- things begin to collapse and the specter of dictatorship was back.

England was perplexed and frightened at Paine's welcome of this dictatorship 'for temporary reasons,' partly because Paine wanted to invade and annihilate the English monarchy. It was as if Paine had learned nothing from France's recent times.

Paine read the reports of the French Constitution of 1795. He had now been out of Robespierre's prison for a year, and had recovered physically from that ordeal. The 'Reign of Terror's' *Committee for National Security* had been dismantled by an administrative coup and a constitution had been written.

"Good, good" he said aloud. "It's the best thing of its kind." In other reports, he learned how the three-part *presidium* had been adopted; the "Directory." The excesses of the terror were gone. The sickening secularism was over. There were murmurs of the return of this and the return of that, but overall Paine was feeling good enough about the direction of the Directory, that he went ahead with plans to invade England and remove its King, 'the plague of the earth.'

But what had been learned? Had France even succeeded in bringing the vote to each male? Was it ever discussed whether that was a worthy plan?

The *vote*. To give the same political influence to the beggar as to the master bridge architect like himself—did that really work? It had an echo of *equality of outcome* to it, and apparently Paine was prepared to over-look this. In the American colonies, where only men who were employed could vote, the belief of the constitutional leaders was not on the equality of outcome, but of *opportunity*. For then the vote would be the *reward* for being enterprising and industrious.

This was not all Paine would overlook about his France in his career to spread anti-monarchist revolution wherever possible. The rumors of dictatorship flew about because the taste for the secularism of the previous period was still on the tongues of the population. The reactions to the churches came back. Bourgeoise customs came back and reactions emerged to them. The richer people pursued fine dining sets and trendy hair styles. Poorer people tried to find ways to set those dining parlors and 'big hair' on fire.

So in a blink, there was a move—a *constitutional* one at that!—to become a 'temporary dictatorship.' Underneath it all, France was still unsettled.

When intelligence of this reached England, "Paine" as a brand-name was seriously in trouble. There was knowledge of a French invasion, raising all kinds of suspicions along the south coast. Any irregularity was investigated by the Admiralty. But now there was rumor of that word 'dictatorship' again.

Paine justified this on the basis of prevention of a monarchy. "Isn't that what we had learned?" he wrote in his monthly political magazine from his re-embraced Paris. "The most important thing is to defeat a monarchy."

>|<

For a few weeks, Elnora kept Millie as one of the children. Mrs. Holford had provided what guidance she could.

"I'm going to take my lead from the apostle here. 'Let him who stole, steal no longer, but rather work, to have something to share with those in need.' If the authorities want to pry into what happened in her childhood and the baby, there is nothing we can do. But she is going to have this deep need to be a mother, which God gives our gender when it is time to bear children, and Millie must have an outlet after this devasting disruption.

"It would be best if she poured her life into your little ones, yet that urge must come by our prayer and gentle hints, not by rules. I mean best for now. Then she will hopefully marry, with all this rough past behind her, and flourish with children as much as her husband can support. Let's pray now—pray that we will be reminded to pray first before all urgings to act and try to 'change' her into what we want, so that she knows it is truly from God."

The ladies continued on in prayer, and Elnora was certain that she had a plan going forward to care for Millie.

Elnora had Millie staying in her own room, apart from the children. One morning, she was in an exceptionally dark mood, unable to dress, but Elnora had seen all that before. It was now that Elnora realized why, at her worst, Millie had been unable to form anything to say except 'Maybe he'll be here.'

What she actually meant was that she hoped her little one might have been found and brought to the orphanage. Elnora didn't tire of her, but she did pray, and she brought her more tea.

In an hour, Elnora walked back in to Millie's room while Pastor Holford was occupying the children, and Millie finally progressed to: "I made the wrong decision. I mean there's a little part to this story I didn't tell you yet. He told me I could either put the child at the back steps of a church, in the dark, where we wouldn't be seen, or into the sea.

"I thought: I will simply get this miserable business over with. No vivid memory on the church porch that would pull me back, no worry of dogs attacking, no vexation that anyone heard anything. Ohhhh, forgive me, God forgive me."

Elnora was now sitting close and rubbing her back, and let Millie lean in hard.

"I thought...I thought Fitz was right: the sudden breaking of the bond would solve all that. Yet here I am, like a salmon swimming back to its source. It could have been this church. Not that it makes any difference.

"Instead, I think of him all the time, and my body seeks him so often..." and there was more sobbing than Elnora could imagine.

"Well, Millie, let me tell you something. I need your help, and I kind of think it might help you."

"You need *my* help? I can't help anyone."

"Just wait til you hear," Elnora continued. "These children here, they've all been on the other side of the 'breaking

75

of the bond.' Truly, in a different way. But did you know, I rotate around with the youngest, crawling into bed with them early in the morning? These young ones here, Millie, they need to feel that and I've seen some of them flourish as they get that kind of attention. And you know I'm not their mother. I just wonder...would you do that for them, too?"

Millie was not rejecting what she heard. She had just encountered the first constructive thing beyond her own grief and self-pity and shame, in a long while. She wouldn't have to be out in society. She wouldn't lose the hope and warmth of Elnora, but she would be taking a step.

> | <

Fitz followed the reports of Paine helping the 'temporary dictatorship' that would prevent the monarchy from returning to power. Paine was his hero.

But he had to be careful, and not merely because of his own unresolved 'business.' It was risky to mention anything about Paine on the south coast, and with the Admiralty listening for anything that might connect Paine's strategy with attacks on its members. He had to take caution of his location. He must stay inland. Not to London but at least away from the south coast.

Paine had said there needed to be 'platoons' of philosophers in England in order for his plan to work. Fitz was on it.

In 1798, Paine was still helping the French and others like the Irish to plan an invasion of England, 'the plague of the human race.' Paine would be the leader of the Revolutionary Government once forces had landed.

But Paine had seriously overestimated support. The British feeling was that it had liberty and security and a representative government, and a system of common law that bound even the King. England therefore would struggle against a French Catholic regime that was seen as decadent, militaristic, superstitious and unfree.

Paine thus became suspect of treason. His magazine *Le Bien informe* was banned.

He continued to 'spit venom' at George III. He warned all other monarchy rulers in Europe that Europe was in revolution.

> | <

After a few mornings of waking early with Elnora to light fires and cuddle the children, Millie began to open up further. She began to see the hard knocks some of them had taken, and the overwhelming plight they were in. She thawed. She realized this was their family, and she had also overheard Elnora telling one of them that they didn't have to worry about moving house 'like last time.' Having slept on boards for months at Brighton, pregnant, she now realized how incredibly valuable it was for these children to actually have beds and clean sheets. She cleaned sheets as though she was a nurse preparing a table for a surgery.

She began to take better care of herself, and of them, and began dressing better.

Each day there was more and more to take on—meals, chores, etc.—but Elnora wisely waited for the right moment about 'going out.'

One morning, Elnora came in to the front room in the morning before the day began, and the fire was going. Millie was standing close facing it, and when she turned to Elnora, Elnora knew something had happened. Millie's eyes glistened but her face was deeply calm and happy.

"He hugged me. I *know* it was Him. He hugged me."

"How do you mean?" asked Elnora, taking her hand.

"You said 'He is a father to the fatherless.'"

"Yes." Elnora squeezed her hand.

"It was a dream, or a trance. It was like every day had come back, Elnora. Every day of my childhood. Every day that I was alone as a docker, He gave back to me. I didn't have to resent it all anymore, because He was my father, even though I couldn't see Him. I haven't lost anything, really."

Elnora waited for more.

Millie couldn't say any more, but she was the happiest Elnora had seen.

Then Millie did add, "I may never find my ma or my da, but I have God now. And I have this place, and all these sweet little ones need love."

"I'm so happy for you!" and they turned and hugged.

Millie had not yet even been outside in the garden this whole time at Bourneboro.

Elnora realized how, during this time, Millie was rebuilding herself, and needed to be given more to do until she took that step of going out unaware and took care of something outside, no matter who might be walking by on the street and saying impolite things. God was at work in Millie and she was on an upward arc. Her questions were better and she was showing that she had accepted that there was all kinds of suffering around and these young ones needed her. She knew that Elnora had a young man in her heart as well, and how that might play out, she did not know.

In a week or two, Millie was actually forming the thought in her mind that this whole place might be the work she should continue going forward, and that she was brought here for that reason. She had some cries, but it was not like it used to be.

There was no word from or about Fitz and that was all very much faded anyway. She had heard that there was still a mystery out there about a missing lightman.

>|<

Fitz had now located as far away as Bondon in Hampshire, and although he kept the appearance of a lowly day-laborer, he was brimming inside with his secret knowledge of Paine's plans. He now had several houses covertly following Paine, and made a plan to circuit to them once a month until the day of liberation arrived.

Down at the coast, he could find news from Sussex in the newspaper. He had a friend in Portsmouth who kept copies for him from past weeks. It had been some weeks now since he had any thought of finding Millie. But then, he had no money to leave at Slickson's for her anyway.

>|<

The energy, brightness and initiative of Martin had made him a natural choice, not only to work on the housing project, but to become a foreman to others coming into the program in the future.

All this was gaining momentum when someone else came into Martin's life. He remembered clearly the day his siblings came along behind him in a hand-held chain on the way to Brighton. Today, while perched at the top of a new home's frameworks, he spotted a string of children, themselves in a hand-holding chain, led by a couple guides, coming by to look at the new works and then visit the pond. He couldn't help but remember the 'march' on which he had led his sisters and brothers.

Leading the little band was the diminutive, thin-haired Millie and Martin loved to see her face, though he also noticed a shift in her eyes from time to time, some dark story over her shoulder.

He took a break and went down to talk.

"Matthew Woodland, several months here at Tilson's Estates."

"Miss Millie, from the Bourneboro Home. Pleased to meet you, sir."

"Ahh, Bourneboro. One of Holford's ministries, like this." He waved his hand over the view.

"Yes."

"I've not noticed you there or at the worship."

"No, I haven't... I'd rather not talk about that." And there was a change in her eyes. "Come along, children."

"I'm sorry, Miss, I didn't mean to pry. I was sent here to Brighton, and that church, by my dying mother. My da died fighting in America. From the distance, your little entourage reminded me of walking to Brighton with my siblings months ago. Now, God has blessed me, and I'm well on the way to mastering new construction. My next brother has been here as well, and my oldest sister looks after the others during the day. 6 of us. We've all come through our rough patch, and God has blessed."

Millie enjoyed every word and nodded and the little ones waddled along, and she looked back again at Matthew with a smile and enjoyed his eyes.

> | <

There was a knock at the orphanage door. One of the older boys opened the door to find Matthew inquiring. The boy went and found Millie.

"There's a man at the door."

Millie approached and smiled. "Good day to you, Matthew. Why have you come?"

"I came to see if there was any way I could help your house on my day off. Perhaps a repair, or a change, or a class for the boys."

Millie's eyes brightened. "I think that would be grand. We do tend to run out of ideas for the boys."

"Well, you can have Elnora reach me at the homes when you decide on a specific."

"Indeed I will, thank you so much."

>|<

"Millie, I've been thinking that we should maybe take a trip back to Uckfield" Elnora suggested.

"Uckfield. Why—do you think he might have some money for me now? I suppose there is something he might want to tell me. I don't know. As long as we aren't riding with a load of fish! He's probably got himself arrested by now, for all I know, all that danger and suspicion swirling around Tom Paine."

Elnora shifted. "What if I went myself? Do you think I'd be able to recognize the woman who sent you this way?"

"Yes, she'd be glad to know I'm doing well, and I should thank her. Just keep it between the two of you. I really don't want any further involvement now."

"I can see that. I think I'll do just that."

"We *could* write a letter," Millie suggested.

"I know, but we're not dealing with a sale of fish here. It's meant to be face to face—though not *your* face. Hmmm, no wonder the Americans got tired of conversations that took 4 months!"

"I'd be happy for her to know that she helped save my life."

5

No Stone Upon Another

Basingstoke, Hampshire

Holford concluded another presentation. In the audience that day sat Fitz. Rather than bolster his repertoire on the nonsense of the Bible, Fitz was astounded at what he heard. Being the expressive person he was, he stood up with a question:

Can you explain the necessity of Christ even if all your claims about his foreknowledge of the desolation of Jerusalem are true?

God was in Christ, resolving the debt of man's sins. We all have our sins. Let's say you have taken innocent life. You may even be in the jail for it. Is there any hope for you? Can heaven forgive something that earth must make demand for? Indeed, it can in Christ, and you will see that it is those of us with such a message who visit those in jail, against all hope.

Summer's face went blank, wondering if this traveled speaker knew something he didn't know. Had the mystery of the signalman been solved and warrants issued? He realized this had been a mistake to show up here and he departed into the evening to reduce his profile again. But then he heard the name Thomas Paine come up in the very next question. He found a shadowy spot below a window of the hall and listened.

Ah, Thomas Paine. Now there's a bright man who unfortunately is making a mistake that shifts the whole picture. We find that there are practical contradictions when modern spokesmen drift too far from the truth of Scripture. Huxley spoke about his doubts about the Bible—and then upheld the Bible's morality for the schools of London! Or "Miss Evans." She left her evangelical upraising, didn't she? Yet she writes painfully of the place to which her departure took her. What line in English literature is more sharp than that of 'the lingering "murder" of a marriage'?

Now in this case, you may be expecting some specific political statement on my part. But I will make none. I merely ask that you know the material of this inflammatory rebellion by these zealots yourself, and its fanatical hold on its God—a hold so close that it was blind to so much of its own evil. We have seen too much of that across the channel. They may try to get rid of God but there will be one, be sure. Or a Goddess.

Fitz was rather stunned by this man's presentations. He wasn't exactly in a political camp, yet he had something to say on each topic that challenged all that Fitz championed.

The real question for Mr. Paine was whether the American revolution was really the sort of thing to take England into the future. There was common law, and it bonded even the King. There was also increasing representation. Most English peasants without any land did not quite get the appeal of the dissenting party about the rich and poor as far as being "created" that way. That was a straw man, as seen by folk who handled quite a bit of the stuff.

Too many things could happen in life that would alter your position. Disease, death, abandonment. There was no direct line back to creation by God like Mr. Paine had depicted and scoffed.

And then there was the admiration of most of these hard-working people for the risks which their landowners took. It was a risk too great for most of them to conceive of.

Again, there was the appeal of 'the vote' as Mr. Paine promoted, which did not quite stack up. These people had mastered agrarian skills, but the property owners had mastered the questions of bargaining, buying and selling. And the risks associated with that. The workers wouldn't have the requisite knowledge to vote on regional issues the way their owners did. The laborers wanted *work,* they didn't want votes.

The idealism of Mr. Paine in bringing the vote to every possible individual simply did not make muster in England. It would be all too easy for political movers to enlist scores of voters who had no business and therefore had no business voting on questions that were the supreme business questions of the day.

So the one-size-for-all of Paine and his local provocateur, Fitz Summers, only had an appeal to those who did not see the hard issues of property use and ownership up close. It tended to appeal to those who had simply read clandestine newspapers more and theorized more. Because they had time to. Paine had missed the target.

>|<

Elnora had put together a more elaborate plan about Uckfield. At first, she thought of just taking a basket or two out there and coming back with them full of vegetables for the home.

But then she prayed that God would provide something even bigger—and more coordinated. A *carriage* out to Uckfield and money to load it with food for the orphanage on the return. While there she would locate the kind woman who had sent Millie to the Holfords.

The answer to this prayer did not come quite as she was expecting. It was just that after one of the Sunday morning services, she was lingering around and talking to her usual friends, but a fish merchant was still in the main room, and overheard something about a 'carriage to Uckfield.'

"My problem is the return; there is no question of going."

"You have your answer then, sir!" exclaimed Elnora. "I need an empty carriage returning and will spend most of the food budget there I think."

"Pleased to make your acquaintance, Miss Picking. Andrew Davies to serve you. There is simply one question—a bit delicate, I think. But can you 'hold' while on a rough ride and surrounded by the odor of a fishmarket?"

"*Hold?*"

"Will you spill?"

"*Spill?*"

"Will you need to *empty your stomach?*" he burst out, a bit embarrassed to have to supply the emphasis on this topic in a house of God.

86

"Oh, I see—but I can pray about that as well!"

"Then can you set a date? I need to know fairly soon, you see."

>|<

As the century mark approached, the relative receptions of Paine and Holford were a huge contrast. The teaching of Holford not only restored a general confidence in the Bible on its historical matters. It was also a fascinating survey of what one radical and fanatical revolution had been like. And that was discussed in the fresh memory of what had happened in the 'other city' as Dickens would write, across the Channel.

Holford had captured the imagination of the English people; Paine had tried to 'sell' an American revolution to a people who had no need for it.

The spies of the Crown were working the French scene steadily. It was learned that the same Thomas Paine was himself involved in plans to invade England and to get rid of the King. "All Europe should be on notice that monarchism is over; revolution will come to all."

These facts would trickle back to shipping offices and pubs all along the south coast.

Fitz would make trips down there, half hoping to see Millie again, half to skulk the streets and detect what he could. He wondered if she had reported him. That led to the thought that he might need to track her down and get rid of *her* before she had.

"I asked you once about your background, Millie, but I thought I might be prying." The couple sat together in between parts of the morning service of Brighton Evangelical.

"Yes, I remember. Well, what can I say? I truly don't have a surname. I really am a child of the docks and the markets. I knew that if I was willing to work as the merchants called for work, that I'd always have some money."

"Well, you didn't have any control over that. You have flourished here, Millie, because you have a heart for children like yourself."

Millie nodded. "There are other things, bitter things, but I learned about Joseph's life recently—the Biblical Joseph. How he had two—" she gasped in air "two children... One of them was named 'To Forget'—meaning he was made to forget bitter things."

"And the other was Flourish—like you, Millie." He squeezed her hand briefly.

She nodded again and smiled.

"I can forget what you forget; I will take care of you if you can't," Matthew added. He was not saying this to 'sound' persuasive. He knew it from the deaths of his parents, one from news 4 months later, and one up close that ended with his mother's smile as she stepped through to heaven.

Her eyes watered, and she nodded again. "I love you, Matthew Woodland."

They grinned but were quiet, seeing if anyone in the chapel heard them.

"When I came here," continued Millie, "Elnora said there must be some purpose to my ending up here."

"Millie, just think of it. How many of these children

like us could we help over our lifetimes? How many could we help come into happy homes which they had invested their lives in?"

"*We?* Do you mean this purpose is something we would do together, that we would marry?"

"It does."

Millie was overwhelmed with joy. Elnora came along, and sensed that Millie had something to say.

Millie leaned into her "I was just hugged again!" she whispered forcefully.

Elnora countered. "Oh, not here, I hope, I mean—"

"No. Remember—that morning, at the fire. *He* hugged me. My childhood was made right. Well, now, my future is right!"

Elnora grinned and hugged her.

Millie went on, aloud to both Elnora and Matthew. "What if everyone in England came to a place like this—this gathering of believers—and find their place in His purpose, no matter what horrid things had happened, and maybe also meet a partner?"

> | <

With word of unsolved assaults on English soldiers going around, there was plenty of interesting chatter, if you knew where to gather it. It was exhiliarating to do so. Fitz imagined himself 'in the big time' now in secret operations, listening under windows of restaurants, impersonating gruff dockmen as he walked tangent to Royal officers on patrols.

He also found information that would keep him trying to hang on to his dream of being a revolutionary instrument. The main piece was that of Paine intending to become the governing leader of a post-revolutionary England; in short, the 'president' of the country. For Fitz, this notion was still the obvious choice of plans; he, like Paine, did not yet know how badly they had missed the English public. Hadn't thousands of copies of Paine's books reach London and been received by certain groups?

But it didn't occur to Fitz that that—a book—was the problem. While there were some receptive spots in some big cities, the mass of the English population was not reading books, but rather reading the news of France. You'd have to be crazy to want the same thing in England!

So while Fitz dreamed of such opportunities as a major role with Thomas Paine in a reborn England, things were going quite the opposite direction for the leader himself. Another trial of a publisher who attempted to spread Paine's book in England resulted in fines and jail.

But even in France, the 'honeymoon' of a Constitution which Paine helped to create was brief. The Directory became a reality—three individuals appointed by a smaller house of representatives to act rapidly with the execution of an individual on certain things. But there were forces from both the revolutionary period and its counter that were affecting the function of this arrangement.

Among the problems for Paine was the ban on his political magazine, produced in Paris, and the spectre of prison again. More disappointing for Paine was the rise of Bonaparte as a monarch, now using the title 'emperor.' There were quite a few angles to the struggle for power and France was not settling easily. It was merely swinging from one near-dictator to another. Quite a bit of what needed to be sorted out in presuppositions and definitions was not sorted out.

As they rolled along through the country toward Uckfield, at triple the speed of walkers, Mr. Davies asked Elnora how her short-term future looked. It was her favorite topic.

"My young man is now trained enough to fill in as a pastor for Mr. Holford while he is traveling so much with his presentation. My father has agreed to the marriage. I will take a break from managing the orphanage, although we have an understanding that changing 'mothers' is just as difficult for the children as them 'moving house.' So my Martin Holford knows we can only set the date when the right person is found for that. And you, Mr. Davies, what do you think of the turbulence Mr. Paine proposes? What is the effect on your work?"

"I have faith that even though some criticisms by Mr. Paine against His *Mad*-jesty are true, that the government will realize what actually works when it comes to taxation."

"Taxation?"

"Some of them think that the Royal treasury must increase tax to increase the balance of the treasury. But in fact, the opposite is true. It is a curious and mysterious dilemma. But if my haulage is taxed too much, I will quit for something else. The increase of taxes only feeds discontent and creates confusing change. The economy is disrupted."

"Oh, I see. It's not something I would know, and that's where I don't see why he—Paine—wants us *all* to vote. Surely there is a sensible person in the offices who can see what you are saying."

"But some of those rousing the mobs want them to feel like they *do* know enough—when they *couldn't!*"

"Yes. Well, tell me something else about your life, Mr. Davies. What has marriage been like for you?"

Davies pondered for a while. Elnora waited. "When you are by yourself, you have one way of feeling all the things life sends you, or *not* feeling—you can just crowd them out; when married, each of them is doubled. The highs are higher, the lows are lower."

"I don't think a woman can 'crowd them out.' They crowd her out! So... you don't regret that you married?"

"I don't. And you are right. Men and women are not identical and never will be. And I don't mean the obvious things. My wife and I may not be as passionate as when we first married, but now we know that marriage was a practical gift from God. Two are stronger than one by themselves, and our children are our security when we get old. We will need them, yet they will also need us for guidance.

"I wouldn't want to go through life alone without a woman's admiration. I know she would not want to be alone for life, to never to receive affection, to never be held."

"So you would say that what you seek most from your wife is her admiration?"

"By far. A man gets down the stretches of life and questions whether he has accomplished enough. I am only a carriage operator, yet my wife always is astounded at my repairs or inventions to improve the equipment or the burden on our animals or the business connections."

"Thank you. I will write that on my heart for my young man."

"Indeed. The young need the old for guidance. And that's true about this 'revolution' matter as well. While 'Tom' the rebel thinks the answer is the stopping of monarchies, what we have learned from the Americans is that to ignore the cries of the people is imprudent. Monarch or no monarch."

"Yes, that is so true."

"And now, supernaturally it seems, Pastor Holford is criss-crossing England with this double blade of his, even though illegal sales of Paine have increased in the cities. The average Englishman is convinced of the sensibility of the Bible and of the madness of revolutions. I met a farmer who had seen the large sketch on the wagon, and Holford had stopped. He had certainly understood about madness: 'If you have an army of 10, and come against an army of 20,000, won't you seek 'terms of peace'?' But the revolutionaries don't seem to consider costs—or know how to count their following!

"But never mind all that Elnora. Back to your new life: what do you think is the most important thing your husband can give you?"

Elnora instantly answered "Honesty—but of course, I've lately been host to a young woman who had received almost none and who wound up on my floor. I'm not expecting to run into a situation like hers! Still, honesty must be nearly at the top of a woman's list. 'Give me a little money so I have something to work with; but don't lie to me about a lot of money just around the corner.'"

"Indeed" added Davies. "Learn how to count!"

>|<

Having raked the area of Ditchling for clues and sitings, the investigator of the Admiralty had finally given permission to the local news publisher for an item about the death of Lightman Carstens:

ADMIRALTY LIGHTMAN RECALLS CURIOUS
FEMALE ENCOUNTER
--Ditchling, Brighton Constabulary.

Abner Pruitt, in His Majesty's Service, was the lightman, during a storm last month, who noticed a woman at the shore below him. He descended quickly in the twilight with his light and believed that when seen half way down, the woman was in the waves with a box of some description. In the minutes it took to reach her, Pruitt could not confirm the object, and the woman was on her way inland and did not assent to questioning. The object was never seen clearly among the waves and rocks, and the receding tide at that beach is something of a menace. She also left the scene with a box which Pruitt believes was distinct second one that night.

Some days later, in the next storm, the body of lightman Benjamin Carstens was found on the rocks below the Ditchling light station. The Admiralty continues to pursue the connection between the two events, both of which happened at the peak of the two storms.

It was yet another week when Fitz was visiting Alton when he came across talk of this item. *Another* lightman in the murky picture of what had happened? How could that be?

He made for Portsmouth where the friend who stored newspapers for him found the short article and read it to him. Fitz was thrown into action--and chaos.

While he was recalling all the details of that night again, he realized he had never asked his 'reader' friend about the weather codes he had seen in the lightstation's log book.

"I need you to look up something for me. I need a list of codes that the Admiralty might use to describe the weather. I saw some one time, and when it came to "AP" and "BC" I had no clue what they were about. See what you can find for me next week when I come back."

>|<

Mr. Davies helped Elnora down from the carriage at the entrance to Slickson's Farm. It was mid-morning after over 2 hours of riding. Elnora stretched and grimaced and rubbed her lower back.

"I expect it will take me a couple hours in the village, then we'll load up here" Davies announced as he left.

Elnora introduced herself to one of the laborers at the farm.

"I'll buy what I can today, at the going price, enough to fill that cart that just left."

"I'm sure the owner will be very happy to see you."

Elnora had some handle on prices as the buyer for the orphanage, but Mr. Slickson was still a bit surprised at the situation here of a young woman out in the country, buying a cart full of goods to take back to Brighton.

He was unaware, of course, that Elnora was looking for one of the women there for a brief word.

"I'll be wanting the sturdier vegetables; they've got to have a stronger back than I!"

"Indeed. What news do you bring from the city? Does the Admiralty think the light system is compromised?"

"Why would they?" asked Elnora.

"The attack on the signalman. It is not solved, is it?"

"No, not solved yet. Otherwise, in the Brighton area, the catch has been good lately. You'll see your cod price is down, I think."

"Thankfully."

After checking through several boxes of vegetables, Elnora was quite pleased how all this was working. And then she rested, and a kitchen laborer brought her tea.

But she had only taken a couple sips when she spotted her target. A woman fit Millie's description and was at a sorting table. "It's delicious!" she told the cook. "What is that woman doing?"

"Ah, that's Kathryn," and the cook stared hard but the shadows were preventing her from a conclusion.

"Nevermind. I'll go see for myself," Elnora resolved after another sip. And approached the woman.

"Elnora Picking, out from Brighton to purchase—to *pick*—vegetables."

"Kathryn Merrimount. Do you have a shop there, then?"

"No, not exactly. But I do need to feed 14 children, now 15. This is a way to economize, as long as the haulage is a bargain."

"Indeed."

"Could I have a word—could we take a short walk?"

"Alright then." Kathryn wiped her hands from her sorting and trimming, and they moved toward a field.

Elnora continued. "I have a greeting to bring you."

"For me?"

"From our 15th."

Kathryn was puzzled. "*From your 15th?*" She looked at the age of Elnora. Elnora smiled, hoping Kathryn would put the facts together and keep the whole picture as secret as possible. It worked.

Elnora added. "*She* made it. She sends her thanks to *you* for steering her our way."

Kathryn gasped and pulled Elnora close. "Oh, I'm so glad to hear. Oh, thank God, that poor thing, she was out of her mind--and out of clothes. Is she improving?"

"Oh, yes, but I only seek to know if there is any concern for her safety at this end—from what you know?"

"Oh, Fitz... We see him every couple weeks. He comes and works a day or two and says his following is increasing. Well, he wouldn't learn anything here, and he doesn't know anything. I haven't told anyone here where she went. Some think she's with him; some say she went off on her own. So don't even tell me where you are exactly, but I don't think he'll ever show himself in Brighton again. He keeps inland now. Too many patrols."

"She'll be happy to hear all this. Take me back to the main house, then. The less talk, the better."

The women nodded and smiled at each other and returned.

The cook warmed Elnora's tea. "Did you work out a monthly buying plan with Kathryn?"

"It might lead to that. You have to keep these things secret you know," Elnora smiled slyly.

6

The Voyage of *The Lonely*

Fitz left the coast that night after hearing the report from Sussex and walked deep into the night. He began to realize how many pieces of his ambitions were now torn apart, and thoughts of Jerusalem's rebels and their cities' building-stones pulled apart filled his mind. No stone was upon another. He was indeed under siege. The way he had treated Millie, the way Paine had misunderstood the societal climate in England, the lack of response, the trial of Williams, the return of France to the monstrosity now known as the Revolution and now this bit of news, which had conclusions only he could provide. It all became very heavy on his soul, on his thoughts, and then on his feet. He was grinding to a halt when he realized that this was the end of all that he had worked on.

There really was no point in continuing. He stood in the middle of a road in the dark with his hands on his haunches, as though he was answering 15 people pressing in on him—or unable to answer them.

And then something truly awful, in his way of thinking, happened. A line came back from Holford. '*What if you had taken innocent life, would you wonder what the purpose of Christ was then?*' He knew he had to flee. But this time it was not the farm country of Hampshire or even Cornwall, as wild and isolated as they might seem. He was not going to become the kind of outcast he had heard of in those parts. He was going to reinvent himself in another country.

He found tall grass by the way and laid down his mat and blanket and tried to sleep a few hours. It felt great to get off his feet which had turned to lead, it seemed to him.

But he was devastated by yet another thought. For as little as he could read, he had always had a great memory of what he had *heard*. Something awful had fallen into place.

"AP" in the lightstation log books was Abner Pruitt, the signalman interviewed in the newspaper about the woman. "BC" was the one he had pulled over the edge to his death. The expressions had nothing to do with weather.

Sleep was ruined.

He wrestled and wrangled on his mat and hated his life, and hated that it was dark right now as he needed to do something, anything. There weren't even stars to look at.

He finally got an agonizingly short spell of sleep. When he woke, he was charged in a new direction that he thought would solve all this. He would first find a disguise and then get over to Southampton as soon as possible. He had noticed a poster in the docks area about another country.

> | <

Paine sat with a writing friend in their Paris location, sizing it all up.

"Tom, you look a bit troubled today."

"I wonder sometimes what has been motivating me."

"How do you mean?"

"The complicated way we got married and then the tragic childbirth—"

"Oh, you're going all the way back to *that*."

"I don't know, I am just thinking that I've had an anger at God this whole time, but the King is the personification of Him, so I direct it at him. I wonder what I would be if I'd had a happy marriage and family. I think I would have put my energy elsewhere, and wouldn't have risked so much on the characters over in France. They've taken one plank of mine and have become so outrageous. Fighting monarchs is not enough of a denominator on which to build."

"It's very hard to see ourselves, to see that we've directed anger at the wrong thing when we are consumed with it" the friend counseled.

"Apparently."

"If a monarch was to slash extravagant spending of 'projected' money, would you praise him? Or if a house of representatives voted unanimously to enforce a state of security that imprisoned you for your magazine, would you welcome that? After all, it was the freely considered *vote*."

"Yes. And no."

"So Tom, you must go back to where you started and balance out your impulses with counter powers. You must do within yourself what you have created in your constitutions."

"Indeed. And yet..."

"Yes?"

"Love had just started to follow."

"Love?"

"For my wife. They—the parents—were right after all. Love was following the decision to marry smartly. And then there was the loss of it all."

"And...did you begin to think that there would never be another woman—even if you began with 'love' instead of from approval by elder guidance?"

"I'm not sure what I thought then. I don't remember if any of them—the senior parties—said to 'try again.' I left. I wanted to put it all away behind me... Now, wait, what did you say, just a moment ago? *'You must balance out your impulses.'* Then I have failed in all this, and in changing England, and losing the public to Holford, because I went for impulse. I could have loved again, but I threw myself into speaking out the disenchantment with the King that I found in the new world. *That* impulse. Oh, sorrow and blindness—to think that loving a woman might have changed me, balanced me; that it really is 'not good for the male to be alone.'"

There was more to Paine's shrunken world, more than can be explained here. He still, for whatever reason, could not embrace Christ who had given certainty to millions against death and sin. Instead, he had his own private reason for 'hoping for a happy life beyond death.' That was as much as he would say about his faith.

>|<

Fitz was going back through Portsmouth when his news collector caught his attention.

"I have that information you need—"

"I don't need it. I figured it out, thank you" he growled.

Taken aback, his news collector moved on. "Also, there's something about Holford. There's a son of that pastor and historian Holford—Martin--and he's to be married. He's involved with their orphanage work in the city and that *em-park-ment.* He's marrying the governess of the orphanage, in fact."

"What's that?"

"A family by the name of Tilson had given some land and put forward some money in trust for building materials. They are also connected to the church—the same pastor. It is a design of several economical houses, built by people apprenticed in a trade, and it's all working fabulously.

"And, oh, it's a double announcement. Now *there*'s economy, har, har!"

"Oh, you mean a double *wedding.*"

"No, it's just saying that the *bridesmaid* of the one wedding is announcing *her* engagement in the same notice."

"The other couple—who are they?"

"Let's see, it's here...It is one Matthew Woodland, now a foreman at the building sites."

"And the girl?"

The friend gave him a dismissive look. It was the look of men when learning that a yet another woman was no longer available for marriage. "It says 'Millie.' No surname. She works at the orphanage. They'll be needing help, no doubt. The orphanage, I mean, not the couples!"

"*Millie?*"

"That is it. What difference is that to you?"

"Nothing, nothing!" Fitz huffed off. His friend sat perplexed at his desk.

After a couple blocks of wandering around looking for a mercantile shop, Fitz stopped with his eyes full of tears at the total waste of his effort so far. He hid himself in an alley for a while as he tried to sort it all out. Then his thoughts turned to Millie, but not to *care* about Millie.

He didn't really care about what had happened to her in all this, but he was trying to figure out what she had done and become. *She's gone back to the area hoping our child somehow survived.* In this, he had a sense that he was pretty close to the truth, yet he didn't know why. Except that he knew he had to stunt all thoughts about the child, and that was why he had ordered her to make a quick abandonment, and would never have chosen the barely-superior option of leaving the child at a church.

But thoughts came. And now he wondered if she actually *had* found the child alive, and the orphanage had taken them both in to recover but the abandonement was all hidden in background that would remain sealed.

He forced himself to get back to his goal of leaving on the first ship.

He passed a mercantile shop with its special notice:

POST HASTE TO ALL ENGLAND

He could write her. But what would he say? He was a failure in every way. Well, there *was* her engagement.

> *Dear Millie,*
> *I have set sail for Argentina, never to return. By coincidence, I found the double announcement in a Brighton newspaper. I wish you every happiness in your new life, and that you can forget our old life.*
>
> *Fitz S.*
> *Portsmouth*

That was how he managed these reckless, anxious days. Two lies to protect him further, and a sparing amount of concern. He intended to feel good that he had tidely closed "it" again.

>|<

Once in Southhampton, he located the poster identifying the ship in need of crew to Australia and of companies seeking laborers there. *The Lonely* would sail in a few days.

Next to *The Lonely* was *The Fox.* It was an entirely different type of vessel and manifest. *The Fox* was to conduct a natural survey of Argentina and the Falklands.

On board *The Fox* was to be a leading naturalist, of course, but also an associate of Mr. Lyell who was the new geologist who had proceeded on the belief that 'the present is the key to the past.' In other words, only processes that we can see going on today are to be allowed to explain the geologic forms we see today. The theory had radical implications for history, for theology, and for the mathematics of calculating time, which few could imagine at the time. Mr. Glipston would be surveying the Rio Vera Cruz valley regarding this.

Fitz noticed a sign at the ramp to *The Fox* that each day at 10:00 until it sailed, there was a short presentation on the mission of the ship and the naturalist and Mr. Glipston the land surveyor on these things.

At first, Fitz—disguised--was surprised to hear the dissent from religion from Glipston that he used to spout out, and wondered if he had been copied. But the speaker went off in another direction he had never heard, and into a contradiction that knocked Fitz off balance:

105

In addition to our finding so much dissatisfaction with religion and church, we wish to say that a new religion is coming—Science. People will no longer be plagued by doubts and fears of the past, nor judgements of the future, because it will rely only on *repeatable* evidence, which is the only rational way to proceed...

His defeats, his sleeplessness, his anxiety about his own future and the upcoming 6 months on the sea overcame his reserve that would otherwise have kept him quiet.

"Man, do you have any idea what you are saying?" And noticing the crowd around him, and concerned that his 'cover' might have been lost or his voice recognized, he receded, shouting "What are you looking at?"

> | <

"How did this ship get its name?" Fitz asked a fellow crew member as they were underway.

"Some islands out there. I forget just where now. Like an invincible explorer, the owner wanted the most difficult feature to be understood from the start."

"What will it return with?"

"Wool if possible, but there is also a breadfruit market and it keeps. Oils. Who knows what else they'll find along the way. I've heard there is something from whales that is more valuable than gold! Just floating around on the surface!"

Fitz had noticed a rather sprite, educated man with a few books. That is, he always seemed to have at least one tucked under his arm. A few hours later, with the south coast still in their view nearby, he introduced himself.

"I intend to be a pastor out there in that country. With all the men starting over in new lives, after criminal sentencing, there will be a need for leadership. There are several on board here."

Fitz looked around. There was no obvious indication.

"So, you must have a Bible."

"Indeed."

"What have you read lately? What did you read today?"

"*The tongue is a flame and sets the world on fire.*"

"Really. How depressing." Fitz departed for work elsewhere on the deck. But something in the water caught his eye. Bobbing in the waves was an object that Fitz strained to bring into focus. But he couldn't give up. At its nearest passage, it became clear that it was a busted-up hand-basket with a cloth snagged to it, wandering aimless in the drifts.

Fitz wretched to think that such a thing could have come right to his attention after all. He grieved over it all, over all the effort, over the waste of his apparent ability to speak to the groups seeking reforms, over what he'd done to Millie and their child, the and dead sailor, over missing Millie's flourishing in a completely different world, over his attachment to Mr. Paine.

He went back and found the young missionary, and clutched him and pulled him along back to the railing to show him. The young pastor was alarmed but kept up with Fitz as they went back.

"There, see, in the water, the busted-up basket, the cloth. I...can't...Just keep that in mind will you? What you saw there. I can't talk about it right now." And he left for his work on the deck.

He threw himself into the work of the deck and he tried again to forget it all.

The missionary wasn't quite sure what to make of it all.

A few days later, Summers was sitting down on the deck below an upper level, with some spare time and a bottle of wine he had brought along for the voyage, nearly full. The seas were now shifting and movement was felt on the decks.

The missionary had taken out a large Bible with nice word-carved covers and had it out on a crate up above, unknown to Fitz, directly overhead. But he had become distracted and left the Bible there.

Suddenly there was an abrupt pitch and the Bible slid off the crate. Down it fell to the level below right on Fitz' wine bottle smashing it and its contents, and falling open.

Fitz sighed and decided to look at where it had happened to open. He could make out the large Roman number 1 and a name that started with a T. The print was in two columns and among the few words he knew from memory was "Christ Jesus" at the top of a column.

"Well that's that" Fitz said looking at the mess of glass and wine. Off he went to get something to clean up with.

He ran into the pastor.

"I, er, have your large Bible. It nearly landed on my head."

"Oh? How do you mean?"

"I'll show you. I'm having to clean up what happened."

They arrived at the spill and the mess.

"Tell me something," asked Fitz, "I can't read too much. But I see this line starts with 'Christ Jesus...' What else does it say?"

Christ Jesus came into the world to save sinners, of whom I am the greatest...

"Who said that, and what did he say it for?"

"Well, you see, that was Paul the teacher of most of the new Christians of his time, but he had formerly been their antagonist. He imprisoned and killed some. When he became a Christian he even left the area for a while and went to another country—"

"To another country?"

"Yes, he had to start over and God had to teach him 'all over again' compared to what he had grown up in."

"Can you do that?"

"To 'start over'?"

"I mean can you teach me how to start over again? I'll start by telling you about the basket and the cloth out in the sea."

The missionary nodded.

Interplans.net develops stories in to feature
motion-picture scripts.

Made in the USA
Columbia, SC
20 June 2024